———————— ★ ————————

Walking across the courtyard a little while later, I suddenly knew, absolutely knew, and without any doubt at all, that the killer had been in the yard the night before. He had seen me and he had heard me.

I didn't know who he was, I hadn't seen him, but did he realize that? With no clue to his identity, or why he had killed the man, I was a blind target. The thought made me lengthen my stride until I was almost running by the time I jerked open the door of my old Toyota.

I'm a good snoop but I don't even pretend to be brave. I'm a charter member of the coward's club, and the idea that I might be the killer's next target had me thoroughly scared.

———————— ★ ————————

Previously published Worldwide Mystery titles by
E. L. LARKIN

HEAR MY CRY
HEAR ME DIE
DIE AND DIE

DEAD MEN DIE
E. L. LARKIN

WORLDWIDE.®

TORONTO • NEW YORK • LONDON
AMSTERDAM • PARIS • SYDNEY • HAMBURG
STOCKHOLM • ATHENS • TOKYO • MILAN
MADRID • WARSAW • BUDAPEST • AUCKLAND

DEAD MEN DIE

A Worldwide Mystery/December 2001

First published by Thomas Bouregy & Company, Inc.

ISBN 0-373-26406-2

Copyright © 1999 by E. L. Larkin.

Printed in U.S.A.

This one is for Jim,
who has *always* encouraged me to write.

ONE

I SHOULD HAVE KNOWN something was wrong the minute I saw the garage door propped open with a rock. Everyone in the building was careful about not leaving those doors open, and as a temporary tenant I'd been told any number of times by the regulars. But I was running late—it was nearly seven—and I had other things on my mind. It was Friday, and although it was already dark as the inside of a polecat, it wasn't raining. I had a new Liz Claiborne outfit and a date with an interesting man. It looked to be a terrific weekend. Which wasn't necessarily the norm for me, nor for Seattle weather in October.

I was staying, temporarily, in a friend's apartment. Her unit is on the ground floor of an old building at the base of Queen Anne Hill, one of the few structures in the district that have survived the current rebuilding craze. The rooms are huge, high-ceilinged and beautifully proportioned. On the down side, the kitchens are purely awful and the electricity is always malfunctioning.

As it was now. All the lights around the back of the building were out. I had to practically feel my way across the patio to the back door and onto the concrete landing where I stepped up the one step. And fell flat on my face onto something soft and squishy that felt unpleasantly like a body.

I felt for whatever had tripped me. "What the heck…?"

My searching fingers found a mouth full of teeth.

Screaming, I rolled sideways off the step and fell into Edith Vibike's flower bed where I scuttled in a circle like a berserk crab. I was still trying to fight my way out of the bushes when Inge Sundstrom from upstairs shoved the door open and the hall light revealed I had tripped over the naked body of a man. A very dead man. There was no possibility of error. Judging from the condition of his head only an optimist would have felt for a pulse. Inge did.

I threw up in the shrubbery, which at least stopped me screaming.

By the time the police arrived I had calmed down somewhat but the next hour wasn't one of my finest. Later, in the apartment, when a Detective Sergeant Tom Neuman from the homicide department asked if I felt better and could answer a few questions, I told him I didn't think I'd ever feel better.

"You'll get over it," he said callously, his attention on a notebook in his hand. "Now, Miss, uh, Dem-ary Jones?" He looked at me inquiringly.

"De-mary," I said shortly. Demary is actually a man's name. I inherited it from my Scot grandfather. He pronounced it Dem-ry. I pronounced it De-mary, but I didn't feel like giving the sergeant a rundown on my family history.

He nodded and went on, "I know you've already told the first officers on the scene how you found the...uh...the victim, but I'd like you to go over it one more time with me while it's still fresh in your mind. Okay?"

I took a deep breath and repeated the story again. It didn't get any better.

"Then what?" the sergeant asked when I

stopped at the point where Inge arrived and I'd first seen the body.

"What, what?"

"What did you do next?"

"I threw up."

"Uh, yes. And after that?"

I rubbed my face, trying to pull myself together. "I don't know what happened after that," I said finally. "Inge helped me out of the bushes, and Ruby Chambers from upstairs came running out and a bunch of other people came. Inge had blood on her skirt, so she went back to her apartment to change and—"

"No, I don't want to know what anyone else did," he interrupted. "I want to know what *you* did."

"I didn't do anything. I just stood there."

"The whole time? You never moved?"

I decided I didn't like this guy, nor the way he was talking to me. I'd fallen over the body, not killed the man. "What are you trying to get at, Sergeant?" I asked. "I tripped, fell on him, screamed, and according to Inge I was still trying to find my way out of the shrubbery when she got there a few minutes later. From then on there were at least ten people around who have a better recollection of what happened than I do. You can ask them what I was doing. I don't remember.''

He looked at me for a minute, his face blank, then said, ''I understand you're a private investigator. May I see your license?''

I got it out of my purse and handed it to him without comment, wondering who had told him I was a P.I. I didn't feel like correcting him or explaining what I really did. I still felt queasy. I had been involved, if involved was the right word, in several murder cases, but this was the first time I had ever had any physical contact with a dead body. I had seen a man shot, and had accidentally been shot myself, but this was somewhat different. Despite having scrubbed my hands until they were almost raw, I couldn't get the sticky feeling of the man's blood out of my mind.

Neuman looked the little plastic card over carefully before handing it back. The written identification was correct—five foot two, one hundred and ten pounds, auburn hair (curly and with a mind of its own), green eyes—but the picture looked more like an orangutan than anything else. I didn't think he noticed the address.

''Miss Jones, according to, uh...'' He

looked down at his notebook again. "According to Officer Hanson you said you had never seen the victim before. Have you thought about that since?"

"Yes. I mean no, I've never seen him. Not that I remember anyway."

"You're sure?"

"Sergeant, I told you, I don't think I've ever seen him before. Nowhere, no place," I said, beginning to get mad. "What else can I say? I was simply the unlucky person who fell over him. And I wish to heck I'd come home at my usual time and let someone else have the pleasure."

"This isn't actually your home, though, is it? Or at least not according to your license. How long have you been living here?"

I gritted my teeth and tried to reply in an even tone. It's a violation of your license to change your address without notifying the board. "I'm staying here temporarily. I've been here three weeks now. The apartment belongs to a friend, Sherry Hall. She's away at the moment."

"Why?"

"Why, what?"

"Why are you staying with her?"

I nearly told him it was none of his business why, but decided it was easier to tell him something, anything, than to argue with him. "My house is being remodeled," I said shortly. "It's full of sawdust and paint fumes." I didn't tell him the reason it was being remodeled—actually repaired—was because a murderer thought I was getting too close to identifying him and had wired a wad of gelignite to the front door.

Neuman gave me a curious look but he didn't pursue that particular line any further. Instead he turned to Inge, who was standing in the kitchen doorway, a mug of fresh coffee in her hand. She wasn't a friend of mine, in fact I didn't really know her or anyone else in the building very well, but Inge had certainly been a friend that evening, cleaning and bandaging the cut I'd managed to inflict on my leg as I fell off the porch, and making sure I was okay.

"You're a nurse, an R.N. Is that correct?" he asked.

She nodded.

"I understand you felt for a pulse as soon as you saw him. Did you detect any sign of life at all?"

"No, none. Actually, I knew he was dead the minute I looked at him. A large portion of his braincase was completely shattered. Obviously his head had been bashed in with some kind of object or weapon. Checking his carotid was simply a reflex action."

"Any sign of body warmth at all?"

"Very little."

"Can you make an estimate of how long he had been dead?"

Inge stared at him. "No, I can't. I'm not a pathologist."

Sergeant Neuman shrugged. "I thought you might have an educated guess, so to speak."

She didn't answer.

He asked her a few more questions and then left without speaking to me again.

Inge made a sour grimace as he went out the door. "That guy has all the charm of Attila the Hun," she said, handing me the still-steaming coffee. "Are you going to be okay, Demary? Alone, I mean. I've got a foldout couch you can sleep on. Or are you going to go home?"

"Thanks, but I'll be fine. And no, I don't think I'll go home. I'm too tired and the place is still too much of a mess to be comfortable.

Believe me, you'll be able to hear me if I need any help. Plus, Edith is right next door.''

"She is?''

"Oh, no…no she isn't. I forgot. She left this morning on a vacation.''

"I wondered why she hadn't joined our merry little group.''

Inge's tone was tart. She doesn't care much for Edith and is obvious about it. Or maybe it's just Edith's type she doesn't like. Not that I suppose they have much contact, but the few times I've seen them meet, Inge was invariably curt and unfriendly. Fortunately, Edith doesn't seem to notice. She is a dithery little blond of somewhere over sixty who never seems to take in what's going on around her anyway.

"Darn, if you live in a big city you know things like this happen. You don't expect them to happen in your own backyard, though.'' Inge covered her eyes for a moment, obviously shaken.

A big woman, tall and heavy-boned, with classic Nordic coloring, Inge works at a skid-row clinic where she frequently sees the results of violence, but as she said, a murder in your own backyard is a lot more personal.

"What I'd like to know is who the heck he is and how he got here," I said, sipping coffee. "He sure didn't come on his own, not buck naked like that. What happened to his clothes? I don't think the police found them anywhere. The killer must have taken them."

"Probably. Or he might have been killed somewhere else and brought here."

"Stark naked? And why naked, anyway? And why here?"

There didn't seem to be any answer to that or to any of the other questions that were going through my head. We talked a while longer but neither of us had anything sensible to add.

As soon as she was out the door I stripped off my clothes, leaving them in a pile on the bedroom floor, and got under the shower. I upped the hot water until I was practically parboiled and stayed there until it began to run cool before I got out. I found a pair of clean pajamas, wrapped myself in an old terry-cloth robe of Sherry's, and went into the kitchen to root around under the sink for the bottle of brandy I'd seen there. The bottle was dusty and brandy isn't my favorite drink, but I thought its fiery strength might cure my shakes. I poured a generous shot in a jelly glass and drank it down like medicine standing there staring at the wall. Afterward I went back and bundled up my clothes to toss in the trash. They weren't torn but they were splotched with blood and dirt. I suppose I could have had them cleaned, but I knew I'd never wear them again.

TWO

THE PHONE WOKE ME at seven the next morning.

"Demary? Demary, is that you?" Martha Kingman demanded.

"Of course it's me," I muttered, trying to get my eyes open. "What do you want? It's Saturday."

"I know what day it is. What I want to know is why you didn't call me last night."

"Call you? Why should I... O-oh, no-o. That horrible dead man." I sucked in a chest full of air as I remembered.

"Have you heard the news this morning?" she asked.

"No. I suppose the whole mess is on TV, though. I saw a couple of cameramen in the yard last night."

"Well, fortunately they didn't get a shot at you. Or at least they don't have your picture on-screen, but the news makes you sound like the number-one suspect.''

''Wha-a-t?'' That really woke me up. ''How could they? I fell over the guy. That's all! I never saw him before.''

I went on to tell her what had happened, complete with gory details. Martha is my office manager, my friend, my confidante, and anything else she feels like being. Black and beautiful, she is an even six feet tall with a figure like a board, Grecian features, close-cropped black hair, and an astringent personality. Born in Barbados, raised in Liverpool, England, and educated at Berkeley, she still speaks with a broad English accent and uses U.K. colloquialisms despite the years she has lived in Seattle.

''What did you say his name was?'' she asked as I finished telling her about Neuman questioning me.

''Detective Sergeant Tom Neuman.''

''Hm-m-m. Have you ever heard of him before?''

''No. I think he's probably a transfer from some other division. He may be replacing Jake, or maybe he's just a temp because they're short-handed with Sam away.'' Lieutenant Sam Morgan, head of homicide, was in Quantico taking some kind of course, but Jake, a longtime friend, had quit Seattle to take a better position with the Snohomish County sheriff's department.

"Well, it doesn't sound as if Neuman actually thinks you're guilty of anything, but it's too bad both Sam and Jake are out of..."

"Guilty of anything?" I yelled. "I fell over the darn body. That is all! He can't possibly think I killed him. I never saw the man before!"

"Don't get yourself in a twist, Demary. I didn't say he did. But if he's going to be in charge of the case it might be a good idea to find out about him. And find out what he said to the reporters. You know how the media is. They get half the stuff they report wrong, and the other half wronger."

"Wronger?"

"Right. But don't worry. I'll see what I can find out and call you later." She hung up abruptly.

I hadn't been a bit worried before. I was now.

Despite having gotten myself involved in several homicide cases—mostly just by asking

questions of some of the people concerned—
I'm not a private investigator. Certainly not
the type portrayed on the television. I'm the
owner-operator of Confidential Research and
Inquiry, or C.R.I. I do all kinds of research for
private parties, mostly writers, but also for law
firms, and for several insurance companies.
They find it cheaper to hire me than to have
one of their staff do the work. I'm better, and
faster, at it if I do say so myself. My main
interest, however, is still genealogy.

C.R.I. was a regular P.I. operation when I
went to work for the original owner, George
Crane. George hired me as office help, a gofer,
and although he insisted that I get my P.I. license he never had me do anything that he
considered the least bit dangerous. He taught
me what I know of the business just from being around him. I'm a natural-born snoop anyway.

After George died—he was killed in a
senseless drive-by shooting—I inherited C.R.I.
by default. George didn't have any relatives
and no one else wanted it, so I put my name
on the door, but I'm not, and never have been,
a real detective. I stick to what I know best,
genealogy and research. Few people realize

how much of their lives are recorded somewhere, and available to anyone who has the
know-how to find the information. Unless you
have never had a social security number, are
very careful, and pay cash for everything you
do or buy—and I do mean everything—you
are on a database of some kind somewhere. If
you are the average citizen you are on record
in at least a dozen places just to start with.
Your birth certificate, marriage license, tele-
phone number, credit cards, utility bills, the
census, any number of mail-order businesses,
credit reports, charity organizations, department stores, license bureaus, and many more.
And these are just the legitimate ones. A researcher who knows his business can find out
a lot about you without your ever knowing it's
been done.

Although they are supportive, it's not a
business that has ever appealed to my parents,
so the first thing I thought of after Martha
hung up was calling them. I didn't want them
to hear some garbled story before I had a
chance to tell them I was perfectly all right,
but then I remembered they had left early
Wednesday morning in their Winnebago to go
fishing at Westport. So unless they decided

to go into a tavern—highly unlikely—they
wouldn't see a television nor hear the radio
until they got back. Both were nondrinkers and
dedicated fishermen. They have always been
good about it, but I know they worry about
me sometimes. I have, on occasion, gotten myself into somewhat dangerous situations. Recently, while trying to sort out a murder case
for a friend, the main suspect had blown up
my house, and tried to get me along with it.
The house sustained considerable damage; I
didn't. Which, as I told Neuman, was why I
was currently living in the Rosario apartment
of my friend Sherry Hall while my house was
being repaired.

My parents are the average middle-class
couple (my father is a retired real-estate bro-
ker) with two children, two cars, and a paid-
for home in the Wallingford district. My
brother has followed in their footsteps. I'm the
maverick. Not that we don't all love one another, it's just that we have different ways of
looking at things. None of my family believes
in making waves. My automatic reaction to
anything that frightens or embarrasses me is
to come up swinging. That embarrasses them.

And by noon I was about to do just that.

Find someone to swing at. Everybody I knew, or ever had known, called to talk about *my* murder. I got very tired of repeating the same things. When my friend Birdie Swallow asked why I didn't recognize the man, I nearly jumped through the phone at her.

"Because I never saw him before, that's why," I snapped.

"There's no need to get snippy about it. I only asked a simple question," she said, hurt.

"Simple? *Simple?*" I could hear my voice rising. "I've been asked that same darn question a dozen times now. I'm getting sick and tired of hearing it."

"Well, you'd better get used to it, and start using your head, too," she said in a regular big sister tone. "You're going to answer a lot more questions before it's over."

She was right. My next caller was Sergeant Tom Neuman. He wanted to talk to me again, and would now be convenient?

THREE

I COULD HAVE SAID no, of course, but I was curious to know what he wanted. He said he was only a couple of blocks away and would see me in a few minutes.

I pulled on a pair of jeans and a violet-colored Fair-Isle sweater, then stood looking out the window as I waited. It was cold out with a weak and watery sun peering through an overcast, but the patio looked quiet and peaceful. I'm an avid reader of detective/suspense novels, plus I do a lot of research for mystery writers, but I couldn't for the life of me think why anyone would dump a body out there. It didn't accomplish anything as far as I could see, and it couldn't have been all that easy to do, either.

The Rosario Apartments are built in a U shape around a beautiful Spanish-type courtyard with the garages along the alley at the open end of the U. The garages have electronic openers for the overhead doors, and although the three inside doors have only simple spring locks, they are never supposed to be left standing open, as the back doors to the main building aren't locked at all. In fact, there are two large printed notices in the garage, reminding the tenants to be sure the garage doors are kept closed. An eight-foot-tall board gate in the wooden fence between the garages and the building gives access to the trash cans and Dumpster in the alley, but it only opens from the inside. The only other access to the courtyard is through the apartment building itself, through the main entrance. The man hadn't been killed on the porch, or at least so I'd heard one of the police say, so how had he gotten there? And if he'd been carried, either through the building or across the patio from the garages, why hadn't someone seen what happened? And why leave him there, anyway? There were several places in the courtyard where a body could have lain concealed for some time. Also the gate to the trash area was only a few feet away from the porch. If the body had been left behind the cans, or even in the Dumpster, it might not have been found for several days.

When I opened the door to Sergeant Neuman's knock he looked so different it took me several seconds to recognize him. Dressed in jeans and a western-cut shirt that made him look like a young James Garner, he wasn't the hard-nose cop I'd built up in my mind. He wasn't particularly handsome, but his brown eyes had beautiful long lashes. Wide-shouldered and narrow-hipped, he had the look of someone who worked out on a regular basis.

"I'm not interrupting anything?" he asked as I invited him in.

"No. Yes. You're interrupting the calls I've been getting from all my friends asking when I'm going to be arrested," I said, motioning him to the cream-colored couch by the window. "What did you tell those reporters last night?"

"I didn't tell them anything. I think the publicity honors belong to your neighbors."

"Which ones?" I asked as I pulled one of the cinnamon-striped chairs around to sit opposite him.

"I doubt it was any one person. The reporters simply picked up on your name because you found the body. Did you think I was trying to railroad you into Walla Walla?" He smiled, showing a set of beautiful white teeth.

"I was beginning to wonder. Particularly when you said you wanted to talk to me again."

"Oh, that. Uh, I was simply in the neighborhood and thought of something I wanted to ask you. Also I'd like to know more about what you do. I understand you own and operate Confidential Research and Inquiry. Is that right?"

I shrugged. "Well, yes. But C.R.I. isn't what you probably think. I have a degree in historical research. I collect, process, and deliver information. My customers are primarily lawyers and insurance companies. I also have a number of clients who are writers, and I do a lot of genealogy work."

"Can you give me an example?"

"Sure," I said, showing off. "Do you know Virginia Martineau? The state senator's wife? She hired me to do a genealogy workup on her mother's family. She hopes to prove that one of her ancestors was on Washington's staff during the Revolutionary War. She wants to join the DAR.'' Neuman didn't look impressed—maybe he'd never heard of Senator Martineau—so I went on. "Last week one of my writer clients asked me to find him documentation on the murder of Alfonso of Aragon, a crime committed in 1500 by Cesare Borgia, Lucrezia's brother. Lucrezia, incidentally, wasn't the wicked witch history had made her out to be. She was a nice woman born into a family of villains. It happens to a lot of people.''

Neuman didn't seem to have heard of the Borgias either.

"Why have a P.I. license, then, if that's all you do?" he asked.

I shrugged. "It comes in handy sometimes." The truth, which I had no intention of telling Neuman, was I kept my license current to bug Lieutenant Sam Morgan, head of homicide. He and I have had a stormy up-and-down relationship for a long time. He does not like my having the license.

"I see."

"I'm not sure you do," I said quickly. The police are fairly tolerant of privates as long as they stay out of ongoing investigations, but I'd be a lot happier if Neuman realized that in this case I was simply an unlucky bystander. "When I went to work for George Crane, the original owner, it was a detective agency and is still listed in the phone book as such, but I'm a researcher, nothing else."

"I think I remember Crane. He was killed, shot in a drive-by incident, about four or five years ago?"

"Yes. Anyway, after he died I changed the business itself, but I didn't bother changing the name. George didn't have any family and there weren't any business assets, so no one cared what I did with the place." I stood up. Thinking about George always made me angry. His death had been so senseless. He'd been gunned down by a spaced-out teenager who mistook him for a rival gang member.

"Can I get you anything?" I asked. "Coffee? A soda? I put coffee on before you came."

"Coffee would be fine."

"Have you identified the dead man?" I asked from the kitchen. "Any tattoos dedicated to Mom, apple pie, or the American flag?"

"No. No ID on him, of course, and we haven't found his clothes. He looks to be about sixty, sixty-five maybe, took good care of himself, so we may get a missing person's report on him.''

I brought the coffee in. "Do you want anything to dilute this with?"

"No, black is fine." He accepted a mug and went on, "What I really came over for I'd like you to think back to the last few minutes before you, ah, got home. Try to remember everything you saw or heard. First, though, I understand that this isn't actually your apartment, that you're staying here temporarily while you're having some work done on your house, but how many people know that? Here in the building, I mean."

"I don't know. I would guess most of them, though. Sherry has been living here for several years. They all know this is her apartment."

"Do you normally get home here about the same time?"

"No. Usually around five. Depends on what I'm doing."

"Did anyone know you'd be working later last night?"

I shook my head, wondering where this was leading. "I didn't know myself. I was working on something and just kept at it until I was finished.''

"Okay. Think back and try to visualize what you saw from the time you turned into the alley. It was dark. What did you see in your headlights?''

I shut my eyes and tried to remember. It felt strange to be on the other side of an interrogation. "As I'm making the turn I see the rhododendrons along the fence across the alley, and on this side of the alley the end of our apartment building, the fence, and then the garages. Nothing else.''

"Nothing out of place? No sign of any person? Nothing at the far end?''

"No.''

"Did you come to a complete stop in front of the garage?''

"Yes. The electronic gizmo doesn't work until you're directly in front of the door.''

"Then what?''

"I drove in, stopped the car, got out and locked it, came up the walk, and fell over the body.'' I opened my eyes, shuddering as I remembered.

"Go back a couple of minutes. Is the garage

lighted? What did you see when you got out of the car?''

I shut my eyes again, trying to concentrate. ''Yes, the light comes on when you press the electronic opener. I can see Inge's car, her space is next to Sherry's, and...oh, the door to the courtyard was open.''

''Is that unusual?''

''Yes. It closes by itself, more or less, but sometimes you have to give it a shove, too. Last night it was caught on a rock. I kicked it out of the way as I went by.''

''What did you hear as you walked up the path?''

''Nothing. What are you trying to get at, anyway?''

He held up his hand. ''In a second. Go back to when you were locking your car, before you started out of the garage. Think. What did you hear?''

I shut my eyes again and tried to remember, but nothing came to me except the usual traffic noise, a kid calling to someone in the distance, and the screech of a nearby door being closed—normal things.

''So, now, what's the point of this?'' I demanded.

"I think the killer was still in the courtyard when you found the body. The time it took you to open the garage door and get out of your car gave him the time to hide, or get away, but I was hoping you could remember something that would give me a clue to who he was or where he'd come from."

My mouth went dry. For a moment I thought I was going to be sick again.

"What...what makes you think that? That he was still out there?"

He hesitated. "Let's just say the medical examiner's preliminary report indicates the body hadn't been lying there long."

"How jolly." I got up and stared out the window. It had been very dark last night and the courtyard was full of places for someone to hide.

"I'm sorry. I didn't mean to frighten you. I've got a couple of more questions, too."

I turned and was about to sit down again when I had a chilling thought. I hadn't seen anyone, but the killer had no way of knowing that. I said as much to the sergeant.

"That's true," he said in a flat voice. "And he may think you did see him. Until we catch him you need to be careful, very careful. The man has killed once; he won't hesitate to kill again. You have a gun permit. Do you carry one?''

I stared at him, appalled. Sergeant Neuman may not have meant to frighten me, but he was certainly doing it. "No! I keep it in the office. It was George's gun." I stopped and thought a moment. "Good grief, I don't remember where I hid the darn thing."

"You what? You don't know where it is?" Neuman sounded as if I had committed a cardinal sin.

I scowled at him. "It's somewhere around. I wouldn't have thrown it in a trash bin."

"I suggest you look for it, Miss Jones," he said, his tone hardening. "It *is* registered to you."

He was right, of course, but there was no need to be rude about it. My temper gauge started rising again.

I stood, and held out my hand for his coffee mug. "Yes, so you said, Sergeant. And now, if you don't mind, if there's nothing else, I have things to do."

He got up immediately, said there was nothing more, and left.

I hate it when someone backs off like that. It leaves me with an unfinished feeling.

FOUR

WALKING ACROSS the courtyard a little while later I suddenly knew, absolutely knew, and without any doubt at all, that the killer had been in the yard the night before. He had seen me and he had heard me.

I didn't know who he was, I hadn't seen him, but did he realize that? I hoped so. With no clue to his identity, or why he had killed the man, I was a blind target. The thought made me lengthen my stride until I was almost running by the time I jerked open the door of my old Toyota. Despite beginning to look like a fugitive from a junkyard, it started, as usual, with a smooth purr, and a few minutes later I was rolling down Mercer on my way back to my own neighborhood, where, if my house was at all livable, I was going to stay. I'm a good snoop but I don't even pretend to be brave. I'm a charter member of the coward's club, and the idea that I might be the killer's next target had me thoroughly scared.

I have a super house. My great-aunt left it to me. She didn't have any children, in fact, she never married, although I had heard she had gentlemen callers. The house looks like a Victorian wedding cake, three stories high with acres of gingerbread trim, scalloped and diamond-shaped shingles, elaborately turned railings on the porches, and a circular window in the gable. All the rooms have ten-foot ceilings with ornate plastered corners, and hardwood plank floors. It does have a few disadvantages, though, including costing a fortune to heat and having only one bathroom, and that on the third floor.

It was also costing a pretty penny to have it repaired, but fortunately I had good insurance.

When I drove up in front, Joey, my teenage alter ego, was standing in the front yard eyeing the progress of the repairs. Joey elected himself my assistant some time ago. He is thirteen, small for his age, thin and wiry, with sandy blond hair, hazel eyes, and an engaging smile despite his mouthful of braces. (Which I think he polishes with some kind of glitter paste.)

He is the kind of kid who not only knows everyone in the neighborhood, he knows every going on in the neighborhood. He's a natural-born snoop, too.

"They're sure not hurrying any," he told me, nodding at the house with a scowl. "They spend half their time standing around drinking coffee." Joey has an interesting work ethic for his age. He believes in eight hours' work for eight hours' pay, with no time off for coffee.

I couldn't see that any work at all had been done since I last saw the house two days before. I knew it would go slowly because so many of the materials—such as the scalloped shingles—had to be specially made, but I thought surely they would have replaced the windows by now. The openings were still covered with plywood. At least the new front door was in place, though, and I could go inside without having to go around to the back. Joey accompanied me.

Inside looked marginally better than the outside. The walls in my office, the hall, and the front room had been replastered and repainted and the floors had been sanded and redone. The new carpets were still rolled up, the new—replacement—folding wooden shutters

that normally cover the windows and the new
windows themselves, plus the leaded fanlights
that go above the lintels, were stacked beside
the cleaned and repaired fireplace. The two
silk-upholstered love seats that go in front of
the fireplace had been recovered and were sitting against the wall covered with plastic
sheeting. On a gray and gloomy day it definitely didn't look welcoming. I didn't go upstairs. The bottom six treads of the staircase
still hadn't been replaced and the temporary
treads were difficult to negotiate.

Fortunately, most of the inside damage had
been confined to the hall and front room. The
house, built in 1905, had been built to last, and
although the gelignite had demolished most of
the outside front of the first floor, the rest of
the place had stood firm.

Joey patted my hand. "It will be as good as
new when they get done," he assured me.

"It better be," I said, suddenly angry, and
close to tears again. Between my house being
blown up and falling over a dead body, I was
feeling very put upon. I was surprised Joey
hadn't mentioned the body. Apparently he had
put the house concerns first—he grasped my
priorities better than I did sometimes—be-

cause he got to the body as soon as we went back outside.

"Have they put a name to the dead guy yet?" he asked, picking on a scabby knuckle as we sat down on the steps. His sweatshirt—he wasn't wearing a jacket—was stamped with what appeared to be a verse in a foreign tongue, accompanied by stick drawings that made knowing the language unnecessary.

I shook my head. "I don't think so."

He gave me a deceptively guileless look. "Worrisome. We can't do much about finding the killer until we know who he wanted dead."

That jolted me out of feeling sorry for myself. "Whoa," I said sharply. "*We* aren't going to do anything about finding the killer this time. It's too dangerous. We'll let the police do their work without any help from us." I'm always afraid Joey will get himself into trouble asking questions in his own neighborhood, and I sure didn't want him snooping around the apartment where he didn't have friends to rely on.

"Your pal Morgan is off on that training course. This new bird may not know what he's doing," he said, totally ignoring my warning.

"You can't rely on someone you don't know anything about."

He was right about that, but I wondered how he knew Sam was gone. Before I could ask him, however, another kid came whizzing by on a bike and Joey hollered at him to wait up.

He leaped on his own bike and went tearing off, yelling at me over his shoulder to take care of myself.

Taking a last look at my poor injured house, I got back in the car and headed for the office, making myself a mental note to have a few sharp words with the contractor Monday morning.

I don't usually go to the office on Saturdays, but I do normally work some at home. I couldn't now and I had a pile of work I wanted to get done. With no one else around, no interruptions and no phone calls, I could get a lot more accomplished than on weekdays. The lights were on and the building was warm so someone was in one of the other offices, probably Anna Carmine, our resident attorney, but I couldn't hear anyone. I automatically checked the answering machine on Martha's desk as I went by and was surprised to see I had a message from Sam in Virginia. I hadn't expected to hear from him at all. He's not much for keeping in touch.

My long relationship with Sam goes back to the days when he was driving a black-and-white and I still believed in flower power. We have had some rocky ups and downs. Most of the time we are on pretty good terms—once we were even engaged to be married—but at other times we are so irritated with each other we don't speak. Right now, though I hated to admit it even to myself, I was wishing he were here to reassure me, to hold my hand, or to just yell at me for being in this mess.

Which he did the minute I returned his call. "Demary, can't you ever stay out of trouble?" he demanded.

I immediately felt one hundred percent better. "What are you talking about?" I snapped back. "I didn't kill the guy. I never saw him before in my life. It's not my fault the stupid killer left him on the doorstep for me to fall over. And how did you hear about it, anyway?"

He didn't answer that. Instead he said, "Neuman is a perfectly competent cop. You stay out of it, you hear me?"

"How can I stay out of it? Neuman thinks I killed him!" I yelled.

"Don't be silly, he doesn't think anything of the kind." He mumbled something else I didn't quite catch.

"What?"

"I said, you stay out of it."

That wasn't what he'd said. He'd said something about talking to Neuman, and that didn't do my already shaky composure any good. I didn't need two male chauvinists discussing me behind my back even if Sam's intentions were motivated by concern. Fighting with Sam on the phone is a losing battle, however; he just hangs up. Instead I asked him how his course was going. He told me about it and we had a few minutes of more personal conversation before we said good-bye. I put the phone down, thoroughly exasperated with him even if he had made me feel better, and mad at myself for wishing he was back in Seattle.

I did try but I got very little work done and went back to the apartment almost as jittery as when I left. The apartment was as gloomy as the day outside. The flowers I'd bought on my

way home Thursday evening were already
drooping in their vase on the coffee table.

Six o'clock finally came; time to take a
shower and get ready for the date I'd remembered—in the midst of everything—to call and
postpone the night before.

It turned out to be a dull evening. The guy
was a lot more interested in himself than he
was in me, and the only time he varied his
narcissistic conversation was when he switched to the murder.

There are times when nothing seems to go
right.

FIVE

I WOKE UP AT 4:00 Sunday morning and couldn't go back to sleep. I knew I was perfectly safe—all the windows had ornamental iron bars and the door was double locked, plus I'd shoved Sherry's desk in front of it—but my eyes still popped open at every creak and groan the old building made. I gave up at about a quarter of five, dressed, and drove over to an all-night diner in Ballard where I ate a toast-and-bacon breakfast, drank three cups of coffee, and read the morning paper.

The death of my unidentified man rated fewer than two inches of type on an inside page. Of course, between the politicians' latest peccadillos—these people seem to have the moral fiber of a cantaloupe—and all the troubles overseas, the front page just doesn't have room for anything as mundane as a simple murder anymore.

The sky was a dull gray, dripping a fine mist that was just short of rain when I got back in my car. A day as dull and gray as the sky stretched in front of me, and it wasn't even 7:00 yet. There was no one I wanted to see, nowhere I wanted to go, nothing I wanted to do. I was feeling so sorry for myself it suddenly struck me funny. Of all the useless occupations in the world, feeling sorry for yourself tops the list.

"Look alive, you idjit," I muttered. "It's Monday in Hong Kong; go get some work done." Which wasn't as silly as it might sound.

One of my longtime clients, Jan Holbrik, was a naturalized American, an Austrian Jew. He wrote children's stories. Gently funny stories about world history with beautiful illustrations, and a lesson in decency hidden between the lines. His stories were fiction but he was very particular that his historical facts be correct no matter how they were used in the story itself. I did a lot of work for him.

He came from Vienna where his family had lived for over a hundred years. His great-great-grandfather had started the family business, a china factory, in the mid-1800s. They produced a very fine porcelain and by the 1920s it was sold all over the world. When Hitler came into power in 1933 my client's grandfather was head of the family and like most Viennese he distrusted the German leader. Over the next two years he liquidated all the family holdings possible, transferring the cash into a Swiss bank, and in early 1935 he sent his youngest son, Jan's father, Paul, to boarding school in England to keep him out of harm's way. In 1938, finally alerted to their danger by *Kristallnacht,* The Night of Broken Glass, when Hitler unleashed Germany's hoodlums on the Jewish population, Jan's grandparents and other family members began to leave Europe, or tried to. Few were successful. The boy in England did not hear from his parents again after Hitler invaded Austria. He received some news of family members through the auspices of the Red Cross, but nothing direct.

In 1945 when Paul returned home he found a Vienna shattered by the years of occupation. His family had completely disappeared, as had all the family friends he remembered. He stayed in Austria for five years, during which time he married and Jan was born. Like thousands of others he tried to trace brothers, sisters, and other family members, but without much success. With the help of English friends he made some effort to reclaim family property, but by then what he was able to document was almost worthless. He had no documents pertaining to the money deposited in Swiss banks other than a letter his father had written to him in England mentioning what he was doing.

In 1950 Paul, his wife, Marti, and two-year-old Jan came to Canada. There were by that time several organizations helping Holocaust survivors and their families find one another. One of them had put Paul in touch with his father's cousin Carl, who lived in Ontario. The man, now eighty years old, had been in France on a business trip when Hitler took over Austria. With him in France had been Paul's uncle, Grogory Holbrik, the family banker, who had been in Zurich at the time of Hitler's Austrian takeover and had made his way to Paris later. Like most, they did not believe Hitler's armies could breach the Maginot Line defenses and as a result were trapped in Paris when the French government signed an armistice on June 25, 1940.

Their escape and final arrival in Canada, or in Uncle Grogory's case, Brazil, made interesting hearing, but got Paul no closer to reclaiming family money. Cousin Carl knew very little about it personally. As he said, "Grogory and his father took care of all banking matters and, of course, at the time we trusted the Swiss banks." He did know that up to the time he last saw Grogory in Marseilles, as they were getting ready to go their separate ways, he still had with him a metal attaché case containing the documents he had brought from Switzerland in 1935.

Paul, Marti, and young Jan moved to Victoria, British Columbia, and finally to Seattle in 1965 and eventually became citizens. With the help of several Jewish agencies they continued to look for Uncle Grogory for another few years, but had finally given up sometime ago.

In 1996, President Clinton signed the War Crimes Disclosure Act. This act made it impossible for the Swiss banks to continue refusing to allow Holocaust survivors and/or their descendants to claim the thousands of dollars they had deposited in secret accounts. Paul and Marti added their names to a class action suit but had done nothing further about finding Grogory.

That's where I came into the picture. Marginally. I don't have the expertise to research international banking, nor was Jan greatly interested in the money, but for his parents' sake he would have liked to find Uncle Grogory. With world interest in the situation building he thought there might be a better chance now of locating him. And that is something I am good at. Finding people. Using the letter cousin Carl received in Canada as a springboard, I had been looking for Uncle Grogory for six months now, and ten days ago I had finally found a trace of him in Hong Kong. His unusual name, Grogory Holbrik, and the fact that I found it associated with a Hong Kong bank, made me reasonably sure I had the right man. So far I had not been able to find anything current on him, however, and I was beginning to fear he had left Hong Kong either before or shortly after the British relinquished the island to China in 1997.

At any rate, working on Jan's problem would take my mind off the dead man.

I worked until 3:00 in the afternoon and then called an elderly friend, Mrs. Ireland, and asked if I could take her out to an early dinner at a waterfront restaurant I knew she enjoyed. She said she'd love it, so I picked her up shortly before 5:00 and off we went.

Somewhere in the back of my head I had the idea that she wouldn't have heard about the murder and I could have a nice peaceful dinner with someone I liked without having to think about the man.

No such luck.

We were no sooner on our way than she asked me how the "case" was going, had the victim been identified, and if not, what was I doing about it. She sounded like Joey. They were the best of friends, so I should have known they would have discussed the "case" very thoroughly. Mrs. Ireland is a darling little lady whose advanced years have sharpened her wits rather than the opposite. Actually, she had been very helpful in solving a triple murder I'd been involved in a year ago, but I certainly didn't want her getting concerned in this one and possible getting herself hurt.

"Mrs. Ireland, there isn't really any case for me," I told her. "The fact that I was unlucky enough to fall over his body doesn't mean I need to have anything further to do with it."

I stopped for a light and glanced over at her. "I don't *want* anything to do with it," I added truthfully.

"You may not have any choice," she said gently. "According to the news broadcast the man was killed elsewhere and deposited on your porch, which means his killer could have still been in the courtyard when you arrived. He may think you saw him, or saw something that would identify him."

I wished people would quit saying that.

"The interesting thing to me is why he was left on the porch," she went on thoughtfully. "There is certainly a possibility that he was killed in someone's apartment and that was as far as the killer got with him before you arrived, but with such a variety of entrances and exits he could very well have been brought there from almost anywhere. Possibly carried from as close by as the next-door neighbor's yard without being seen at that time of night. I'm sure the police forensic experts will be going over all that, though."

"What do you mean, a variety of entrances?" I asked, frowning. "There's just the front door and the garages. Unless you count the gate to the trash cans."

"Oh, no. Joey checked. Besides the three

back entrances and the front door, there are two fire exits from the building, although why anyone would haul a body through the building and then leave it on the porch I can't imagine. More important is the little garden gate at the end of the walkway behind the laundry. The gate not only opens directly into the courtyard and has nothing but a simple catch, it is quite visible behind the shrubbery at the sidewalk end in front of the building. If the body was brought to the area by car his killer could have parked right beside the walk and carried him on into the courtyard with very little chance of being seen at all.'' She paused, tilting her head to stare out the window. ''The why of it still escapes me, though,'' she said.

Horns honked behind me.

''I think the light has changed,'' Mrs. Ireland said sedately.

I wanted to stomp my feet like a two-year-old. I felt like a fool. Of course the building had fire exits. That at least was the law. Why hadn't I checked? And the garden gate. Again, why hadn't I looked around, checked the place out? Sam was right. As he had told me innumerable times, I wasn't a detective.

''It really is a most dangerous situation for you, dear,'' Mrs. Ireland went on. ''You need to be very careful until the killer is caught.''

SIX

BE CAREFUL. Easy enough to say, but by Monday morning I was as skittish as a Mexican jumping bean. Forty-eight hours of starting at every sound, peering over my shoulder constantly, and waking every few minutes all night long hadn't done me any good. The lack of sleep alone was ruining my disposition, which wasn't all that even anyway.

Plus I'd had an uncomfortable time with my parents when I finally reached them late Sunday evening. They were horrified, thankful I was all right, and certainly supportive, but somehow gave me the impression they thought I could have handled things better. Just what I could have done wasn't clear. It was one of our usual conversations. Their perspective was always somewhat different than mine. It rarely bothered me at all but this time it rankled and I had to work at keeping my temper. Which wasn't helped when my sister-in-law called a few minutes after I talked to them. Mostly Cissy is a darling. Unfortunately she is also bossy, and the fact that she is usually right doesn't endear her to me. Mike lets her shove him around unmercifully. Sunday she was determined I should come stay with them until the murderer was found and put away. As I had just gone this same route with my folks I wasn't in the mood to listen quietly. Even if I'd liked the idea I would have turned her down. For one thing they lived in Monroe, a small town northeast of Seattle and more than a two-hour drive from my office, on a *good* traffic day. And that was via a stretch of highway some motor magazine had called the most dangerous in the country.

When I mentioned this she immediately decided I should also quit work for the duration. It took me a good half hour to convince her I intended to go my own way. She wasn't too pleased with me.

Late Monday morning I was putting my jacket on, getting ready to leave the office for a trip to Bellevue, when Jodie Dunham came in. I had my back to the door and didn't hear her until she asked me where I was going.

Squawking like a demented chicken, I whipped around to face her and managed to fling my jacket over her head and out into the hall.

"Watch it! What in the world is the matter with you?" she demanded, backing up.

"Don't do that!" I yelled. My heart was pounding so hard my eardrums hurt.

"Do what?" She yelled back. Jodie is always ready for a slanging match.

I sat down abruptly—fortunately there was a chair there—and covered my face with my hands. "I'm sorry, Jodie, I didn't mean to yell," I mumbled. "It's just that I'm climbing out of my skin and I didn't hear you come in."

She shook her head. "Good grief, Demary, you *are* nervous. I didn't realize it bothered you that much. Are you all right now?"

"Yes, of course, you just startled me." Jodie, her real name is Marjorie, is twenty-six, a law student at the U of W, and is presently clerking for Anna Carmine, who has her law office in the same building as mine.

Jodie is pretty, not spectacularly so, but still very attractive. She also looks like a complete flake with long, brightly enameled nails, heavy makeup, the latest in trendy clothes, and different-colored hair every month. Jodie is nothing like she appears, however. She carried a 4.0 grade average—fantastic for a fourth-year law student—and is unbelievably street-smart for a girl who has grown up in a highly conservative socialite family. Today her hair was pink—not strawberry blond, but pink. Her skirt and shirt were in brilliant shades of red.

"Just because Tom Neuman thought the killer might still have been in the courtyard doesn't mean he was, you know," she said as she went out and picked up my jacket. "And if he was, maybe he hung around long enough to hear what you said and knows you didn't see him."

I had retold the entire story to Martha, Anna, and Jodie when I first came in that morning.

"Maybe. But Inge tried to keep people away from me, especially the newsmen," I said, wishing now that I had stood on the step shouting out my total ignorance of any and all knowledge.

"Inge? How come? She's one of the tenants there, isn't she? Is she a special friend of yours?"

"No, I hardly know her, but she's a nurse and she could see I was pretty shook up." I shuddered. "I still get sick every time I think about it. She got blood all over the front of her skirt when she knelt down to check his pulse."

"I thought you were supposed to be a hard-boiled detective. Just don't think about it, then it won't bother you."

"In the first place I have never claimed to be any kind of detective, let alone a hard-boiled one. You've been watching too many old Bogart movies. Besides, it's a whole lot easier to say not to think about it than to keep it out of your mind. I keep seeing his head, all smashed and bloody, whenever I shut my eyes."

"Yuck."

"Yes."

"Where are you off to anyway?" she asked, changing the subject in a hurry.

"The Mormon Family History Library in Bellevue. I'm working on a family history for Virginia Martineau."

"No. You must be kidding. She's having you do a tree?"

"Yes. What's so strange about that?"

"Nothing, I guess. It's just that she's such a loser, the quintessential name-dropping social climber. Always going on about some movie star she met in Palm Springs or some big-time golfer she and her husband played with at Pebble Beach. I wouldn't think she'd take the chance you'd find out one of her ancestors was hung as a horse thief or something."

"How do you know her?"

"Oh, I don't, not really anyway. She just belongs to the same country club Daddy does and I see her in the clubhouse all the time. She plays a rotten game of golf, never breaks a hundred, and cheats besides." She turned to go, her scarlet skirt flaring around her knees as she passed Martha on the way in.

"What's wrong with your phone?" Martha demanded. "Carol Ann is on the line. She said you'd left a message for her to call, but I couldn't..." She pointed. I'd knocked my cordless set off its base onto the floor, probably at the same time I'd thrown my jacket at Jodie.

I picked up quickly. Carol Ann Guginsberg is a friend who works at the Seattle P.D. "Hi,

Carol Ann. Thanks for calling back. Have you heard about what happened at my…"

Carol Ann laughed. "In detail. Everybody except maybe Neuman thinks it's the funniest thing they've heard in a month of Sundays."

"Funny!" My voice rose.

"Serves you right, Demary. You're always sticking your nose into something that's none of your business and this time you nearly got it chopped off."

"I didn't do anything of the kind," I snapped. "I fell over the guy."

Carol Ann laughed again. "I know, Demary. But you have to admit it *is* a kick. For once you're right in the middle of a homicide, not just playing around the edges."

Carol Ann has a primitive sense of humor, to say the least.

"Anyway, I checked on Neuman like Martha asked," Carol Ann went on. "I talked to Charlie Bacon; he's head of personnel. He didn't seem to be terribly enthusiastic about him but he said Neuman had a good record. Said he was a regular bulldog when it came to questioning a suspect and would use anyone or anything when it came to making his case. Never anything illegal, just rough around the edges. According to Charlie, his main problem is he doesn't have much imagination.''

"Imagination?"

"Charlie says he's too linear, gets an idea into his head and won't consider anything else until he's forced to. Only works on one thing at a time. Personally, I don't think he'll make it in this division."

"Is he married?"

"Married? What difference... Hey, you interested?"

"No, don't be silly, of course not. I barely know him, and what I do know I don't like. I just wondered."

"Me thinketh thou dost protesteth too much."

"Protesteth?"

"Wait till Sam hears. He's the one who suggested Neuman be brought into homicide while he was gone."

"Don't you dare!"

"I'll ask about wives, present, past, or possible, next time I talk to Charlie," she said, chortling gleefully as she hung up.

SEVEN

AFTER I GATHERED the notes I needed to take with me to Bellevue I called my contractor again. He had not been "available" when I called earlier, nor had anyone been working on my house when I went by at 9:00 that morning.

He was in his office this time, and took my call, although I had a feeling he did so reluctantly. After exchanging greetings I started out with what I thought was a reasonable enough request, asking why no one was working that morning and why the work wasn't progressing any faster.

"Are you having some kind of difficulties with materials?" I asked.

He gave a little chuckle. "No, not at all. Everything is fine and we're moving right along on schedule, Miss Jones," he said. "I'm

and tell them what I thought of their bookkeeping.

Meanwhile, being careful obviously wasn't
working. Waiting for the police to track down
the killer was making a nervous wreck of me.
I needed the guy found.

Although I'm the first to deny I'm a P.I., I
am, in a sense, an investigator, and I'm a good
one. Everyday I look for, correlate, decipher,
and sift all kinds of information. The police do
the same thing trying to solve a homicide.

Most sources of information—libraries, genealogy organizations, government records—
are available to anyone with the time and skill
to use them. Some, such as city, state, and fed-
eral records, take patience to unravel, but the
information is there for anyone who knows
where to look and has the ability to dig it out.
In fact, there is an appalling amount of personal information out there about you, whoever you are. And that's just in the public do-
main. Private data banks, such as mailing lists,
credit reports, and personnel records, contain
a whole lot more, all of which is available to
an experienced computer operator with a mo-
dem.

I thought it out after I went to bed. In this

particular case I wasn't equipped to track down the killer. In the first place I didn't have access to the technical tools that might identify him—such as traces left on the victim's skin—but with any kind of a starting point I could certainly check out the victim. Which might give me the motive for his murder, and that could lead me to one or more suspects. Suspects, alibis, motives—those were the things I was good with.

CAROL ANN CALLED ME the next morning and gave me my starting point. "I talked to one of the guys on the Rosario case a few minutes ago. I'm not on it, but I got the dead man's name for you," she told me.

"You do? Who is, or was, he? Tell me," I demanded. "Was he local? When did they…"

"Give me a chance, will you? I'll tell you what they have, but it isn't very much." She paused, rustling papers. "In fact, considering that it's been nearly four days since he was killed, they don't know much of anything."

"Well, tell me! Who was he?"

"His name was Hiram Marcus Taylor. He applied for a driver's license on August 23, 1950, in El Paso, Texas, and has renewed it regularly ever since. Five foot nine inches tall, brown hair and eyes, weight one hundred and sixty-five pounds. Born in Cimarron County, Oklahoma, on January 5, 1922 to William Joseph and Nadene Marie Taylor.''

''That's it? That's all they know about the man?'' I couldn't believe it. With all the manpower, computers, and so forth the police department had available, they should certainly know a lot more than that.

''Sorry, sweetie. That's it. That's all they know so far, except for forensic details. Taylor's body was extraordinarily clean, even under his fingernails. The scrapings didn't turn up anything but soap. He had a recently healed injury to his left forefinger requiring stitches, was in excellent health, and was bludgeoned to death with the traditional blunt instrument. You want to hear about that?''

''Good grief, no. I saw him, and that was more than I wanted.''

''Funny thing. One of the guys said the medical examiner's description of the murder weapon is: 'A smooth, arrow-shaped blunt instrument measuring four to five inches at its widest point.' Can you think of anything fitting that description?''

"No. I don't want to think about it at all. But if they know his name, why don't they know anything else? Address, family, whatever?"

"Beats me. But knowing you, you'll be able to tell Neuman all about him by this time tomorrow. You've got his name and birthplace; that should be enough. Hiram Taylor is all yours."

It was enough. Between us, Martha and I had produced many a twenty-page dossier from far less. I'm good with a computer but Martha is better. She *thinks* like a computer.

We started with William and Nadene, tracking from Hiram's birth in 1922. I worked until 3:00 that afternoon when Tom Neuman called and asked if I'd like to have dinner with him. Just something simple in the neighborhood. I was surprised but I accepted with pleasure.

From a shaky beginning that Friday evening, Tom and I had progressed to a wary acceptance of goodwill on both sides. This was the first time he'd asked to see me again but we had talked on the phone twice. Ostensibly, the calls had been to ask a few simple questions and to ask if I was okay. The dinner invitation was different.

He had never volunteered any information about the investigation and I hadn't asked, but today I could hardly wait until we were seated in the little Chinese restaurant, the Half Moon Café, near my office to tell him what I'd learned.

"I've got some real information for you about Hiram Taylor," I said as soon as the waitress took our order and left.

"What? Demary, what have you been doing?" he asked. His voice sharpened. He sounded exactly like Sam when he reached across the table to grab my hand. "You can't go around talking to people about a murder victim. The killer could be anyone—the guy on the corner, your next-door neighbor, anyone. It's dangerous."

I couldn't believe it. What was the matter with these guys? I liked the concern in his voice but even if he didn't know me very well he should know I was no hot dog. I hastened to reassure him. "Not people, computers. I've only talked to four live people all day, and all of them were out of state. What I've done is gather background on Hiram. Some of it's pretty interesting."

Tom started to say something but was interrupted by the waitress coming back with a pot of tea. After she left he asked, "What do you mean, interesting?"

"We-ell, to start with, considering what I've found out—or actually, not found out—I'm not sure that it was Hiram on my doorstep."

"Don't be silly. We matched his thumbprint with the one on his Texas driver's license."

"Uh-uh. What you matched was the thumbprint of a man who *said* he was Hiram in 1950. When he was supposedly twenty-eight. How many twenty-eight-year-old males do you know who don't have a driver's license?"

"You don't know that he didn't have one previously."

"Well, if he did it was in a foreign country, because he was never issued one in any other state. And he was never issued a passport, so I don't think he was ever out of the country."

Tom eyed me thoughtfully as the waitress deposited cups of egg-drop soup in front of us. "All right, I'll admit it's a little strange," he said when she was gone. "But that doesn't mean he wasn't Hiram. What makes you think…?"

"Let me tell you, from the beginning. All right?"

He shrugged.

"Okay. William and Nadene, Hiram's parents, were married in 1921. She was thirteen, he was sixteen."

"Thirteen and sixteen?"

"She was expecting a baby and back then, particularly in Oklahoma, if you got a girl in a family way you married her, regardless. Six months later, Hiram came along. When Hiram was two months old they set out for south Texas, hitchhiking."

"How do you know that?"

"William, or Billy Joe as he was called, was arrested March second in Amarillo, Texas, for stealing a bottle of milk off somebody's back porch. Nadene, the baby, and the hitchhiking are all on the old arrest report. I have a friend near there in Del Rio, New Mexico, who got the Amarillo authorities to fax me a copy. The charges were dropped, probably because the milk was for the baby. A month or so later Billy Joe went to work as a roughneck for Basin Oil Company out of Hockley City, Texas. He and Nadene were included in a city population count made the fall of that year when the town was in the process of being renamed Levelland. William Joseph and Nadene Marie Taylor. No Hiram.''

Tom made circles on the tabletop with his teacup. ''I'll admit that's interesting,'' he said finally. ''But it doesn't mean Hiram was dead. They were kids and they were broke. They could have left the baby with one of their parents, or even put him up for adoption.''

''Possible, yes, but other than his birth and the Amarillo incident I can't find him documented anywhere before 1950. No school records, no nothing. After 1950, yes. I found plenty on him in Texas and Arizona and a couple of other states, but nothing between 1922 and 1950. Doesn't that strike you as peculiar?''

''Yes, and no. I mean, yes it is peculiar, but there could also be a simple explanation. He could've been adopted and not known it, then when he did find out he started using his real name again. Considering the year, 1922, a family may have just taken him in and changed his name without ever doing anything about it legally.''

Our waitress arrived with our dinner and I leaned back to give her room to put the plates

down. We had both ordered moo goo gai pan
with pork fried rice. It looked wonderful and
smelled even better. "Wait till you hear all of
it," I told him.

"There's more?"

"Certainly. That wasn't much more than an
hour's work." I bragged, grinning at him. "I
do this for a living, Sergeant."

Tom smiled back at me. "And you're good
at it, right?"

"You bet your bippy." Between bites I told
him the rest.

Sometime, between 1922 and 1928, Billy
Joe and Nadene moved west to Eureka, California. I located them there on September 10,
1928 with Billy Joe's death. Six months later,
on March 1, 1929, Nadene married Peter Vernon Walker. On July 20, 1930, Nadene's second son, Robert Vernon Walker, known as
Bobby, was born. In 1934 Nadene and Peter
bought a house on D Street, in 1936 Bobby
started school, in 1942 the Walkers rented out
the house on D Street and moved to Alameda
where Peter went to work for Kaiser Ship-
building. Christmas of 1948 saw Peter and Nadene back in Eureka. Bobby, then eighteen,
stayed in Berkeley where he had started fall

quarter at the University. In July of 1950 all traces of Bobby disappeared. In August, Hiram applied for a driver's license in El Paso.

When I finished, Tom took a swallow of his tea, staring at me over the rim of the cup. "Have you got a motive for this disappearing act?"

I shrugged. "Could be anything, but I'm guessing it was Bobby's grades. His grade point average that spring quarter was one point four." I paused for a sip of tea, waiting for him to ask me how I got that particular bit of information. Student records are usually unavailable without the student's express permission. I had a good lie ready but I didn't want to use it if I didn't have to. Martha still has friends at Berkeley and I didn't want to chance getting them into trouble. Carol Ann had told me she didn't think Tom knew anything about a computer—other than as a word processor—and it looked as if she was right, so I went on. "He was flunking out and likely going to be drafted. The Korean War was heating up. The United Nations had asked for troops to restore order and President Truman had just approved ground and air strikes against North Korea that June."

Tom was dubious, but he admitted that if neither Hiram nor Bobby had ever been convicted of a felony the dual identity was possible. "Actually, Bobby at sixty plus would fit the medical report a lot better than Hiram does at seventy plus," he said. "I'll run the prints again tomorrow and see what we get, but in the meantime let's forget ol' Hiram and go bowl a couple of games. All right?"

I was ticked off that he didn't seem to appreciate what I'd uncovered, but I hadn't been bowling for a number of years and it sounded like it might be fun, so I agreed.

Hiram wasn't mentioned for the rest of the evening but he wasn't forgotten. Not by me, anyway.

EIGHT

FOR SOME REASON, once I had identified Hiram, put him in context so to speak, I was nowhere near as jumpy. I didn't forget there was a killer out there, and that he might have his eye on me, but I could deal with it.

"Don't be daft," Martha said sharply when I told her how much better I felt. "You don't know but what the crazy chap's just waiting for his chance to get you alone."

"Well, thanks a bunch. That makes me feel a whole lot better," I said, giving her a sour look.

"Well, I hope it scares the heck out of you. You need to be careful," she said, flouncing back out of the room. She twitched the new quilted wall hanging straight as she went past. It was a mariner's compass done in gold, blues, and grays. She didn't like it, and I had to admit it didn't go well with the two tan-

gerine-colored chairs against the opposite
wall.

I decided I'd better get some work done on
Virginia Martineau's tree and started roughing
out a letter to Lloyd's of London. Lloyd's has
shipping agents all over the world and keeps
meticulous records. It serves as a shipping information agency and also publishes *Lloyd's
List,* the oldest daily newspaper in London. I
was hoping they might be able, and willing, to
give me some information on the Bellinghams.
If the Bellinghams were big enough cotton
merchants to have had their own ships.

I had just finished and was wondering—I
had never thought to ask—if the cotton branch
of Virginia's family were northerners or south-
erners, when Tom called.

"You were right," he said. "It was
Bobby's body. Robert Vernon Walker, born
July 20, 1930, in Eureka, California."

I didn't say I told you so. Crowing is such
bad form. "Does he have a record?" I asked
instead.

"Yes, and no. He was never convicted of
anything, but he was named in a couple of
complaints."

"What kind of complaints?"

"We've got four reports of women, older women, accusing him of conning them out of a chunk of money. None were able to prove it, however, and the charges were dropped. This was between 1962 and '64 in Los Angeles. Since then he's apparently been going straight."

The years rang a bell somewhere. I was starting to ask for exact dates when I was interrupted by a knock on my door, followed by Martha coming in accompanied by one of the biggest men I've ever seen. He was at least six foot six and must have weighed three hundred pounds. He was dressed in a fuzzy brown tweed suit that made him look like an enormous teddy bear.

"Demary, this is Agent McBride, Sean McBride," Martha said, frowning. "He wants to talk to you."

I told Tom I'd get back to him and put down the phone.

"You could have finished your conversation," McBride said politely, holding out a leather folder with a gold Treasury Department badge pinned on one side and his photograph on the other.

"That's all right." I gave the badge and picture a cursory glance before I handed it back. With his dark brown eyes and almost blue-black skin, he made an interesting picture. I motioned to the tangerine-colored chair by the desk.

"The call wasn't important. Sit down. What did you want to talk to me about?"

Martha remained standing. "You don't have to talk to him if you don't want to," she said, scowling at McBride who had sat down and taken out a notebook and pen. "You can, but you don't have to. I brought him in because he...he's married to my old roommate. When I was at Berkeley."

"You don't need to explain me," Agent McBride said mildly.

"Get on with it," Martha snapped.

I blinked, wondering what in the world was wrong with her. She might not be the easiest person in the world to get along with sometimes, but she wasn't normally rude.

McBride turned to me. "I'd like to ask you about the ten thousand dollars that was deposited to your account in the USBank a week ago on Friday evening," he said.

"Is this some kind of a joke?" I asked, looking at Martha.

She shook her head. "No. No joke. Sean is a Treasury Agent. He knew I worked for you. But you still don't have to answer his questions. Maybe I'd better go get Anna."

"What for? I didn't deposit any ten thousand to my account. Not then or at any other time. But what if I had? What business is it of the Treasury? My finances are cert—" I stopped in mid-word as I remembered my bank statement. I'd meant to call the bank and straighten it out, but I'd forgotten.

Agent McBride looked at me calmly. "Yes?"

"My bank statement. I just remembered. I...that's silly. I mean, it was a computer error, a bookkeeping error. Where would I get that kind of money?"

"That was my next question."

I scowled at him. "As I said, it was an error. But so what? It's none of your business how much money I have, or how I get it. You're not the IRS."

"For heaven's sake, doesn't the Treasury Department have to observe the Miranda law?" Martha demanded, practically snarling at McBride. "I told you I didn't think she'd mind answering a few questions, but I didn't say anything about bashing her about.''

"What are you talking about?" I asked, confused by Martha's belligerent tone.

McBride didn't answer quickly enough to suit her. "The money was counterfeit, and McBride here is trying to trace it. He knows perfectly well you didn't deposit it; the bank records are time-stamped eight thirty-two p.m. You were answering questions for Tom Neuman at eight-thirty that night."

"I didn't suggest that Miss Jones did deposit it."

"Will someone please tell me what the heck is going on?" Between the two of them— Agent McBride's attitude wasn't threatening but his size alone was intimidating—I was getting flustered.

McBride sighed. "Martha and I don't see eye to eye on some things," he said with a sudden, smiling flash of teeth. "Actually, on most things, but that's beside the point. First we, that is the Treasury Department, would like to know if you recognize this handwriting." He handed me a photocopy of a bank deposit slip with the date, the word *cash,* and the figure 10,000 printed on it.

I shook my head, staring at it with disbelief. It was certainly one of my deposit slips but the handwriting, or printing, could have been anyone's—including mine. "No, I don't—can't—recognize the writing. Just one word like that, how could I? It isn't mine, though." I handed the photocopy back. "I thought the statement was a typo or something. I meant to call the bank and straighten it out but I forgot. It never occurred to me it might be real. A real deposit, I mean. Now you say it was counterfeit money. How was it deposited?"

"Dropped in the night depository at the branch down the street from the apartment you are staying in."

"I've never used that branch. Anyone could have done it, though." The night depository at that branch was around the side of the building and behind a screen of shrubs. "But I meant what kind of bills? Even if it was all one-hundreds it would still be a wad."

"Yes, it was. And as such was immediately scrutinized most carefully," Agent McBride said. "And as I said, we know you didn't make the deposit. What we'd like to ascertain, of course, is who did. Does anyone else ever make deposits for you?"

"Certainly. Martha does all the time. But we use the branch here by the office. Almost all my clients pay by check, so..." I stopped and looked at Martha. "I don't remember anyone ever paying cash. Do you?"

She shook her head.

"Have you any idea how someone got a hold of this slip?"

"No, I can't imagine. And I never use those little deposit slips out of the back of my personal checkbook anyway. We always use the long forms we get with the business-size checks we use here in the office."

"Trash," Martha said.

"What? What's trash?"

"No, *in* the trash," she said. "Someone could have found one of your deposit slips in the trash. I always leave the deposit slips in the back of the little book of checks when I throw mine out. You probably do, too."

I thought a moment. "Actually, I can't remember doing anything with them, so I probably do." I had a sudden memory of Edith and I chasing our respective trash around the courtyard of the Rosario a week or so before. We had been talking and bumped hips as we went out the back door, scattering debris for the wind to take all over the yard. "I know when someone could have," I said. I told them about it.

McBride nodded. "Yes, in the trash, that's possible. Very foolish, though. Anything such as deposit slips, credit card receipts, or statements should be torn into several pieces before being put into a trash bin. Anything like that can be used by someone with criminal intent. Also, do you have someone in to clean the apartment?"

"No. I do when I'm at home, but not the apartment?"

"Does anyone else have a key?"

"Yes, several people that I know of. Maybe more. You do know it isn't my apartment, don't you?"

He nodded. "Yes, Martha told me."

"One of my neighbors has a key, also the landlord, Sherry's mother, and whoever else she may have given a key to."

"Which neighbor?"

"Edith Vibike. She lives in the apartment next to Sherry's. At the moment I have a key to her place, too. She and Sherry exchanged keys for when they're on vacation, or when Sherry is out of the country on a photo shoot.

They water each other's plants, pick up the mail, that kind of thing. In fact, Edith is gone now and I'm doing the watering."

"When did she leave?" McBride asked.

I rubbed my forehead, trying to remember. "I'm not sure. A week or so ago. No, on Friday. The morning before I fell over the body."

"But she could have entered your apartment and taken a deposit slip out of your desk anytime you were out? As could your landlord, or the parents? Correct?"

I smiled. Suspecting any of Sherry's conformist family of handling counterfeit money was so far off the mark it was funny. "Yes, of course, they could have done so, but it's highly unlikely," I said, getting myself back in line. "What was the point, though? Why would anyone do anything so silly? Some kind of a practical joke? I mean, in a bank? The teller would be sure to spot it. Unless it was especially good?"

Martha answered. "No, it wasn't particularly good. The teller spotted it almost immediately."

"And why my account?" I asked, frowning as I finally, belatedly, began to recognize the implications involved in the situation.

"Somebody doesn't like you," Martha said. "First they leave a body for you to find, then they dump funny money on you."

I gasped. The idea wasn't at all funny.

"I'm only kidding," she said quickly, turning to McBride. "There's no connection, is there?"

"Not as far as I know," the agent replied, shutting his notebook in which he had been making notes during the conversation. "As Martha suggested, using your deposit slip may have been a happenstance. We can't be sure of that, however, and whoever did this had no way of knowing you would have a cast-iron alibi, either." He smiled. "Unless the murderer made the deposit. Which leaves us with your question. Why was it done at all? If it was intended as a practical joke it was very ill advised. The perpetrator faces a stiff sentence, regardless of his intentions. Counterfeiting is a serious crime."

Having just been involved in helping uncover an international counterfeiting scheme, I was well aware that it was a serious crime. As was Martha, which no doubt was responsible for her unusual rude behavior.

McBride left shortly after that. Martha

stayed. Among other things, she wanted to know how my dinner with Tom had gone. Her interest was purely business. She never inquired into my personal affairs, although I usually did keep her up-to-date. Tom was the first man other than Sam that I'd even had a cursory interest in for a long time, but I wasn't ready to admit that yet, not even to myself. I told her what he'd said about our findings, which annoyed her. She thought he should have been more appreciative. So did I.

"Aside from it being a particularly stupid practical joke, which I don't believe, can you think of any reason for that deposit?" I asked, changing the subject and going back to the counterfeit bills. "I mean, why me?"

Martha shook her head. "Somebody playing silly, maybe." She reached across the desk and touched my clenched fist. "Don't worry about it, Demary. Sean is a lot sharper than he makes out. He'll track it down. He's actually on a different case at the moment, something to do with tracing Holocaust survivor money that was held in Swiss banks, but his boss wanted him to check out the counterfeit because it came from the same plates he encountered on another case last year."

"I thought you didn't like him."

"What gave you that idea? I like Sean fine. Charles and I see a lot of them. It's his job I don't like. The government sticks its nose into too much of our lives, and has too much power to do so."

After she left I went back to framing letters to shipping agents but I couldn't keep my mind on what I was doing. The counterfeit money bothered me. Depositing it in my account was such a malicious act. Deliberate. Intended to cause me trouble. Who disliked me that much?

NINE

MARTHA CAME BACK a minute or so later. "Demary, I heard you say something to that cop on the phone about the body not being who they thought. Or the other way around. What was that about?"

"We were right. It wasn't Hiram. It was his brother, Bobby, half-brother actually, Robert Vernon Walker, born in 1930."

"Well, if the body was Bobby, why couldn't we trace him after 1950? Where's he been all this time? And where's Hiram? Were both of them still alive, up to last week anyway, or was Hiram already dead? And if so, why didn't we find any record of his death? Or were both of them alive and using whichever identity happened to suit them at the moment?"

"H-m-m. Good question," I said, thinking about it. "As far as I can tell we were only tracking one man, but we could be wrong. We need to do some more digging. In fact, we need to do a *lot* more digging. This could even be a case of fratricide.''

''Not much joy in that idea,'' she said, and went back out.

I sat and stared at the wall. Identifying Hiram, or actually Bobby, although I continued to think of him as Hiram, seemed to have raised more questions than it answered. At the moment, however, I had something else on my mind.

I had received a letter and a fax that morning in answer to two of my queries about Grogory Holbrik that I didn't know what to do about. Normally, the minute I turn up any important information I give it to the client. That's what I'm paid for. I was reluctant in this case because I knew it was going to be very hurtful. Still, I didn't have any choice and I'd already put it off long enough.

Jan answered on the first ring. He must have been sitting right beside the phone.

''You've found him?'' he said. ''Really? Really? I can't believe it. We've been looking for so long, I... Where? Where is he? Is he all right? Does he—''

"Hold on," I interrupted. "I think I've found him all right, but it isn't all good news, so don't get your hopes up."

"He's dead? No, oh no. What..."

"Jan, do you suppose you could come over here? It's hard to explain on the phone."

"Yes. I'll come right away." He hung up with a crash.

Jan didn't live far from my office but he was still there before I expected. He must have broken several speed laws on the way. I motioned him to a chair and told Martha to field any calls.

"Before I get to the information I received this morning, let me tell you something else," I said as soon as he was settled. "For the last week or so I've been wondering if the man I told you I located in Hong Kong wasn't someone other than Uncle Grogory. He seemed to be too active for someone who must be over ninety years old. The name was right and I had a direct trace from Brazil to Australia in 1961 and then to Hong Kong in, I believe, 1970, when by my figuring he would have been at least seventy years old. Today I got this." I handed him the fax.

He read, frowning. "Is this in answer to a request for a reference? It says Grogory Holbrik was an excellent employee and was employed by the New Territories Bank for fifteen years. I don't understand. Where did you get this?"

"Where I got it isn't the point. Do you realize what it means? If this refers to your uncle it means the bank hired him at seventy and that he continued working for them until he was nearly ninety, and if I'm reading this fax correctly they still consider him employable. And I don't think that would be at all likely if he was over ninety years old."

"You found someone else by the same name? No, it must be his son. Yes? Yes, that must be it. That would be wonderful," Jan said, his whole face lighting up.

"No, hold on, I don't think it's his son, or anyone else related to you. I think the man I traced to Hong Kong is a complete fraud. He could be claiming to be Grogory's son, but I think it more than likely that he's using false papers and is claiming to be Grogory himself.

He could have doctored Grogory's papers to fit his own age and description."

"Why?" Jan asked, puzzled and a bit angry. "Why do you say…"

I handed him the second document I'd received in the morning's mail. It was a copy of a death certificate issued in Miami, Florida, on January 3, 1960. It attested to the death of one Grogory Maarten Holbrik, resident of São Paulo, Brazil, who died in a local hospital of pneumonia. No parents or occupation were listed. His birthplace was given as Vienna, Austria, but no birthdate. Grogory had probably been very ill by the time he reached the hospital—pneumonia is a sneaky disease—but at the bottom of the page in very small letters, someone had written, *patient said no living relatives*.

Jan stared at it for a long time before handing it back. "Are you sure…? Yes, of course, it must be," he said finally.

"Reasonably sure, yes. I talked to passport authorities in Brazil. They told me he had applied for a visa to visit the U.S. in 1959. Miami is a frequent destination for Brazilians. I tried it first and got lucky." That wasn't the whole story but he didn't need to know the nitty-gritties.

Jan stood up, then sat back down. "Why would anyone be using his name? He wasn't famous, or wealthy."

"I don't know why. I can make several guesses, but they would take time and money to unravel and that isn't what you asked me to do." I felt sorry for him and his elderly parents. I had met Paul and Marti and they truly seemed more interested in finding a lost relative than they did in claiming the money that was rightfully theirs.

Jan stood up again. "I'll talk to my father," he said, shaking his head. "But I don't think they will want you to do any more." He put out his hand. "Thank you, for what you have done."

I shook his hand and escorted him out. I'd send him a complete report, but I doubted that he'd want me to go any further. Personally, if I were him, I'd want to know a whole lot more. Such as what had happened to the attaché case Grogory had in Marseilles; did the man in Hong Kong have it, who was he, where and how had he acquired Grogory's identification, and where was he now?

I hesitated for a moment and then told her the whole story. I knew she could be trusted not to pass it on. Bankers as a whole are about as closemouthed as they come, and Susan was particularly so.

"I don't really know anything about him, nor why he was invited here," she said slowly, frowning. "But I can find out. It can't be anything too confidential. And I do know someone who was at the dinner, Chris Patterson. I can ask her about the dinner in a gossipy way. Will that help?"

"Anything might help. I don't even know what I'm looking for really. It's just that I don't like the idea that this man is here, in the Northwest. If he is impersonating the Holbriks' uncle, Paul and Marti could expose him as a fraud. Of course, he may not know they are in Seattle." I shrugged. "And he may not even be the same man at all, the one who went from Brazil to Australia, to Hong Kong, and so forth."

Susan gave me one of what I called her "banker" looks. Narrow-eyed and speculative. "He must know the banking business. He wouldn't have been able to fool those Hong Kong sharpies for long. What you think is that

he has already made a claim on the Holbriks'
Swiss accounts, or is about to do so. Right?''

I nodded. ''Right, and if so the Holbriks, all
of them, could be in danger.''

''In danger? That's a bit melodramatic.
Sounds to me like he'd be the one in danger,
of prosecution for fraud.''

''Exactly. And if he's a violent type, what's
he going to do? Especially if there is really a
lot of money involved, which I have an idea
there is.''

''You've got murder on your mind, Demary. Bankers aren't the violent type.''

''Don't kid yourself. Bankers aren't a breed
apart. If this guy has spent as much time as I
suspect on this fraud, he isn't going to share.''

SUSAN CALLED ME at the office just before I
left for home.

''I just picked up a bit of gossip for you,
nothing specific about Holbrook, though,'' she
said. ''Chris happened to call me about something else, so I asked her about the dinner. She
said it was dull as dishwater except for one
funny incident. Some silly woman who was
seated at another table decided she wanted to
sit next to Holbrook and changed the place

cards. Nobody realized what she'd done at first and they got her back to her own table before the speechifying, but the funny part was she shouldn't have been there at all. She was supposed to be at another banquet entirely. And to Chris, the even funnier part of it was, she wasn't some blond bimbo trying to hit on him, she was a dithery old gal who didn't seem to have any idea what all the fuss was about.''

Something about Susan's description pushed a button.

''Did the lady have a name?'' I asked.

''Yes, and no. Chris only heard part of it and all she could remember was that it was an old-fashioned one. Esther, Edna, Edith, something like that.''

Blond, dithery old gal, possibly named Edith? Could there be two of them in Seattle? Now that really would be pushing coincidence to the wall. But what possible interest could Edith have in Holbrook? I had talked to her on Thursday, the day after the dinner. We talked about the plants she wanted me to water, and surely if she had been at the dinner she would have mentioned it. She always prattled on about everything she'd been doing lately.

I sat thinking for a minute.

Prattle on, she did, but only about the most inconsequential things. Never anything of any importance, and I had a feeling that if she had been at that dinner it was important.

She certainly seemed an unlikely suspect for anything murky, but maybe I'd better take a harder look at Edith.

TEN

WEDNESDAY EVENING Richard Bellam was arrested and held for questioning in the Hiram Taylor murder case—both the police and the newspaper were still calling him Hiram. The desk clerk at the Edgewater Hotel where the police discovered Hiram had been staying identified Bellam as one of two people who had visited Hiram during the week before his death. In addition, Bellam lived in the Rosario—apartment 201—and had an arrest record for passing bad checks.

Martha brought me the news, a cream cheese bagel from the Bagel Factory on Latona, and a cup of Kona coffee as soon as I got to my desk Thursday morning. She was wearing an absolutely gorgeous sack dress in multicolored stripes that looked as if it had been hand woven. Made my mouth water.

"Carol Ann called about him just before you got here," she said.

"Do they have any idea why?" I asked between sips of the hot coffee.

"Why what? Why he killed Hiram?"

"Yes. What was his motive? I don't know the man, Bellam I mean, but I have seen him around the apartment a few times. Seems a mild kind of a guy, not the type to bash anybody's head in."

"People thought Ted Bundy was a nice guy, too. At any rate, that's all I know. That's all Carol Ann told me. She was in a hurry."

Later Carol Ann, who has a cavalier attitude toward departmental information, told me that Bellam had a rap sheet several pages long, but claimed he'd never seen Hiram anywhere at anytime. He said he'd been at the Edgewater to see a woman of ill repute who worked out of the bar there. The hotel management denied there was any such woman, of course, but the bartender supported Bellam's story inasmuch as he did remember Bellam having a drink in the bar with a woman. The police apparently had no real case against Bellam, though, because they released him late that same evening, a lot quicker than I would have thought

possible. It looked as if he had powerful
friends somewhere. Bellam continued to be a
suspect, however. He didn't have an alibi for
the time of the murder, nor, strangely enough,
did anyone else who lived in the Rosario.

Everyone in the building was either alone
in their apartment, or, if elsewhere, without
anyone who remembered seeing them.

Although they were the most logical suspects, the police hadn't been able to establish
a connection between Hiram and any tenant.
Several, including Edith, were supposedly out
of town, but there was no actual evidence that
they hadn't been in the building when Hiram
was killed.

That afternoon I started looking into the
background of Hiram's California record.
Tom, to my surprise, had sent me a copy.

The victims in all four cases claimed Hiram
had stolen a large sum of money from them
using such a hoary old confidence trick I had
a hard time believing anyone would fall for it.
Each of the women said Hiram had repre-
sented himself as a bank examiner and had
asked her to assist him in trapping a dishonest
teller. On his instructions, she had withdrawn
a substantial amount of money from her ac-

count and taken it to Hiram, who was waiting in a nearby parking lot. There he supposedly marked the bills with a special ink, returned them to the bank envelope, and sent her back to redeposit them.

He had, of course, switched envelopes and she was left with a bundle of cut newspaper. And Hiram had not only used the same con each time, he had used it on the same type of woman.

Martha came in a few minutes before 4:30 and told me she was leaving. She and Charles, her husband, were going to a formal dinner party being put on by one of the theater groups at the U that Charles took an interest in. Charles teaches at the University of Washington. She had her dress over her arm—she'd retrieved it from the dressmaker earlier—a black chiffon affair in several layers that looked simply stunning on her.

With her tall, board-thin figure, she'd probably look great in a potato sack, I thought enviously as I asked if they had fixed it all right.

''I think so.'' She held it up for me to inspect.

The eight-inch triangle tear in the skirt, inflicted by the neighbor's cat when it mistook one of the gauzy flowers around the hem for a mouse, had been mended so expertly I couldn't tell where it had been.

I worked a while longer after she left and then headed for home myself. I was still a couple of blocks from the apartment and had just turned uphill from Mercer, when I saw Joey dart across the mouth of an alley and disappear behind an old building that had once housed a commercial bakery.

Or, at least I thought it was Joey. I slammed on my brakes and made a turn around the next corner looking for the back of the building, and the kid, whoever he was, but I didn't see anyone his age at all. This wasn't a family neighborhood. Also it was getting on toward dark, which made it hard to separate figures from shadows.

I went as far as Kinnear Park, cut back on Olympic Place, and crisscrossed another couple of blocks before I gave up, telling myself it couldn't possibly be Joey anyway. He wouldn't be foolish enough to be snooping around here so far from home at this time of night. At least I most certainly hoped he wouldn't.

Tom called Friday afternoon and asked if

I'd like to have dinner again, this time at a seafood restaurant on the waterfront. I had intended to call him that evening; I had some news for him. Telling him at dinner would be better.

I got back to the apartment early enough to do a load of clothes. Inge Sundstrom was taking her clothes out of the dryer when I got to the laundry room.

"I haven't seen you for a while," I greeted her. "How are things with you? You look tired."

"I've been working extra hours. One of the other nurses is down with the flu. How are things going for you?"

"Okay. Nothing new. At least nothing that tops a dead body."

She smiled. "Got over your shakes?"

"More or less. Can't say I've completely forgotten, but..." I shrugged the subject off. I still didn't like thinking about Hiram's smashed head and wondered how Inge could deal with the blood and gore she saw everyday. The clinic where she worked was in one of the toughest sections of Seattle where shootings and stabbings occurred nearly every day.

"No use dwelling on it," she agreed. "These things happen." She took the last of her clothes out of the dryer and shoved them down in her basket.

Smiling to myself, I kept my face carefully blank as I said good-bye. She hadn't been quite quick enough to completely conceal the men's briefs she'd shoved into her basket. I wondered why she bothered to try. If she wanted to do her boyfriend's laundry I certainly didn't care. If it had been me I would have told him to do his own skivvies, but to each his own when it came to love.

THAT EVENING I waited until we were seated, then sprang my surprise with a smart-aleck remark that fell as flat as the proverbial pancake. "Hiram must have had a fixation for tall, blue-eyed blonds in their late fifties," I said. "All his marks were the same type."

"Probably just coincidence," Tom said absently, scanning the menu.

I soldiered on. "Uh-uh. I think he was following a pattern. I called and talked to a Detective Sergeant Adams who worked the case. He's retired now."

That got his attention. "You did what? You

can't do that kind of thing,'' he said, frowning at me. "Darn, I never should've shown you that report. You're interfering in an ongoing murder investigation.''

"I'm what?''

"You heard me. You're interfering in an open homicide case.''

"I am not. I'm a private citizen asking questions of another private citizen who happens to be a retired police officer,'' I said, caught flat-footed by his attitude. "You didn't object to my investigating Hiram before.''

"That's baloney, and you know it, Demary,'' he said angrily. "This is entirely different. You've got no business talking to a Los Angeles police officer, retired or not. Not only are you going to get yourself into hot water, you're going to have me swimming right alongside you.''

The attack—for that was how I viewed it— was so unexpected I didn't even get mad, at least not for a few minutes. He had no right to be so judgmental. It was an unexpected facet to his personality that I hadn't really seen before. One I didn't like. I wasn't doing anything dangerous and I was not interfering in his case. I was doing nothing more than asking

questions about complaints that were nearly
thirty years old.

And not only that, he sounded exactly like
Sam and that not only made me mad, it made
me realize how much I missed the guy.

However, I didn't want Tom to call Adams
himself—I'd told the L.A. detective a few un-
truths—so I swallowed my annoyance and
made an effort to smooth things over. Which
made me angry with myself.

"I asked Adams about the women, nothing
else," I said. "He interviewed all of them."

"Why?" Tom demanded. "What have
those women got to do with what's going on
now? They must all be in their eighties by
now, anyway."

I shrugged. Charlie, the head of personnel,
was right. Tom didn't have much imagination.
"I don't know how, but I think the women,
what they are like, is somehow important," I
told him.

The waitress came to take our orders just
then and by the time we got back to the four
confidence victims we had both recovered our-
selves. Tom seemed to have forgotten his
pique entirely.

"Well, what did Adams have to say?" he asked.

"He said all four women were so much alike they could have been sisters. He said it was actually kind of spooky. His word, not mine. According to him they were all attractive airheads, with more money than brains, and prime targets for a con man. He didn't seem to feel the least bit sorry for them and, in fact, appeared to think they deserved what they got."

"They probably did."

"What?" I could feel the blood rushing to my head. "That's like saying a girl deserves to be assaulted if she's out after dark."

"I don't mean that. Of course they didn't deserve to be robbed, but, so help me, some of these confidence victims are so silly it's almost impossible to feel sorry for them."

"Silly? Silly?" My tone was shrill. Fortunately the waitress brought our orders right then.

We both sat silently, waiting for her to leave. I couldn't believe I'd understood him correctly.

"I think we'd better talk about something else," Tom said stiffly when she was gone.

I agreed. I was so angry I was afraid to speak at all, let alone discuss the case with him. However, by the time he took me home I realized it was probably concern for my safety, not sheer cussedness, that motivated him, so I asked if he'd like to come in for Kahlúa and coffee.

He said he would.

"I've got to take care of Edith's plants before I forget again. I haven't watered them for three days," I said as we walked down the hall. "Here. Why don't you take my keys and go on in and put the coffee on."

He shook his head. "No, I'll wait for you by the door. Make sure you're all right. I still don't feel good about these apartments. The security is too loose."

I didn't argue. I'd gotten over the worst of my nervousness, but as he said, the apartment security wasn't any too good and I could still see Hiram's bloody head in my mind's eye every time I let myself.

Edith's apartment was dark, but I didn't bother switching on any lights until I got to the bathroom. Edith had collected all her plants in the tub where they were easy to deal with, and as her apartment was arranged exactly the same as the one I was in, the light from the hall was enough to find my way around without any problem.

I finished the watering in record time and was starting back toward the open front door when a tall, dark figure, arm upraised, came out of the bedroom.

I screamed. The oncoming figure screamed. Tom came racing into the room yelling, "Freeze! Police!"

Trying to get out of his line of fire, I tripped and did a back flip onto the floor. The dark figure had more sense. She stood still and snapped on the lights.

"It's Edith!" I shrieked.

Edith sat down abruptly on the nearby couch. "Oh, oh my word, Demary, you scared the tar out of me," she gasped.

I sat where I was and tried to catch my breath.

"I take it you're Edith Vibike." Tom holstered his gun and helped me to my feet. I'd tripped over her suitcases.

"Of course I am. Who are you? Good grief, my heart's still going like a trip-hammer." She pushed her fair, baby-soft hair back off her face and fanned herself with the other hand. "Are you all right, Demary? You took a nasty spill."

"I'm okay, just shook up a little." I introduced Tom but didn't bother telling her how I knew him. "I'm sorry I frightened you. I didn't realize you were home."

"I got back a couple of hours ago. I was so tired I just dumped my suitcases and lay down for a nap. I didn't even take my clothes off." She tugged at the leg of the form-fitting aqua jumpsuit she was wearing. Edith had a fantastic figure for her age. For any age. She worked at it, though, going through a complicated exercise routine every morning in front of her TV.

"Still sorry, but I guess we'll both survive."

She brushed my apology aside. "It was my fault. I should've left a note or something."

We talked for a few minutes longer, until Edith and I had calmed down, then Tom and I left.

"Nice lady, have you known her long?" Tom asked as I let us into my apartment.

"No, only a couple of weeks."

"What does she do for a living?"

"Nothing that I know of. I don't think she

ever worked. I understand her husband died
about ten years ago and left her quite well off
cashwise, plus I think she has done well with
investments. She's not the dumb blond she
looks. Why?''

Shrugging, he sat down at the tiny dining
table and watched me put on a kettle of water.
"No reason, just wondered. Where did she go
on vacation?''

"She said she was going to head south until
she found some sun.'' I measured coffee into
my French-press pot. I love French-press coffee; it has an entirely different taste.

We didn't discuss Hiram again that evening.
In fact, we had very little more to say to each
other at all. Tom left without even finishing
his coffee, apparently still ticked at me.

I didn't care. In fact, I was glad to see him
go. I was still annoyed over the way he'd acted
at dinner and couldn't help wondering if it was
concern for my safety that motivated his behavior, or a private concern of his own. I was
beginning to sense a side to him that I didn't
like very well.

Plus, I wanted to rethink what I knew about
Edith.

ELEVEN

I WOKE THE NEXT MORNING thinking about Tom's unreasonable attitude. He was worse than Sam, and if he continued to be so unbending our friendship wasn't going to prosper. The only progress made in the case so far had been through my efforts. If I hadn't identified Hiram for them the police wouldn't know yet who he was, let alone that he had arrived in Seattle six weeks ago via Alaska Air, or that he had rented a car from Hertz and been staying at the Edgewater Hotel. All of which they had discovered only after I'd given them a name.

I certainly wasn't looking for a police commendation, or even any thanks, but neither did I think I needed to be called a silly little fool, as Tom had done at one point during the evening. And the more I thought about it the an-

grier I got. I decided it would serve him right
if I went out and solved his case for him.

I was brushing my teeth when that particular thought went through my head, resulting in
my spraying Aquafresh bubbles all over the
bathroom mirror laughing at myself.

I really was being silly now. I didn't have
any idea what Hiram had been up to in those
six weeks, nor any way of finding out without
running afoul of the homicide department.
And without Sam here that could land me in
big trouble, and Carol Ann, too, if she kept
feeding me department information. Plus,
without some idea of what Hiram had been
doing, where he'd gone, who he'd seen, I
didn't have much hope of finding his killer.

Or do I? I wondered, staring at my spattered
reflection. I knew as much about the case as
the police did, or close to it, and I probably
knew more about Hiram than they did. Tom
had told me everything he found out, up to
last night anyway, and Jodie had continued to
be interested in the case, too. She had talked
one of her father's friends who was in the state
motor vehicle department out of the license
number of Hiram's hired car. Not that the
number had gotten me anywhere, at least not

so far, but one never knew what bit of information might lead to something.

I stood running a comb through my unruly hair, wondering what was the matter with me. I'd never been so afraid to make a move before. Maybe it was the memory of the smashed head, the blood all over my hand, that was making me so timid, but whatever it was I'd better get over it.

Deciding what I needed to do was organize and collate what I did know, I washed off the bathroom mirror, pulled on a pair of old jeans and a Seahawks sweatshirt, and drove over to the office, passing my house on the way. To my immense satisfaction, there was a full crew working. On a Saturday.

Joey hailed me from the corner. I pulled to a stop at the curb to let him get in.

"Joey, were you over by the Rosario last night?" I demanded immediately, before he even had the door shut.

"Yep. Learned a few things, too," he said complacently, scratching his tummy. He was wearing a denim jacket and a ragged T-shirt that left several inches of skin exposed. What I could see of the shirt bore what looked suspiciously like a seminude male figure spouting steam out of its ears.

"Joey, no, I told you to stay out of it," I said anxiously. "You don't know anybody over there. You can't go around asking questions. The killer could be anyone. You'll get yourself hurt."

Somewhere at the back of my head I had a faint memory of someone else saying the same thing to me. I brushed the thought away and frowned uneasily at my teenage pal.

He gave me one of his exasperated looks. "Not likely. I got more nous than that. I only talk to people I got a handle on. You want to hear?"

I did.

"Okay, then. You know that restaurant down on Queen Anne, almost to Denny Way, called the Cornerpost?"

"M-m-m, yes. I think so. Pretty upscale."

"Right. Well, I got myself acquainted with one of the busboys there. He told me Hiram had dinner there with a lady the Saturday before he was killed."

"He did? Did the boy tell the police?

"No. An' he won't, neither."

"Why not?"

"He lied about his age. He's only thirteen. He'll lose his job, an' he needs the money. Bad. He's big. Looks plenty old enough."

I thought about that for a minute. Washington has very strict child labor laws. Should I report him, or not?

"He only works two days a week," Joey added, looking at me out of the corner of his eye.

I nodded. I wouldn't say anything. There was a lot of trust involved here, plus Joey had been careful not to tell me his name.

"How did he know it was Hiram, and what was the woman like?" I asked.

"Heard her call him by name and thought it was a weird one. That was the only reason he remembered them when I showed him Hiram's picture out of the paper. He's Vietnamese, or part anyway. Not too many Vietnamese kids named Hiram."

"Could he describe the woman?"

"Naw, not really. Said she was a big blond, that's all he noticed." He hesitated. "He thought he'd seen her someplace before, though. If he remembers he'll let me know."

Hiram seemed to be choosing the same type of woman right up to the end.

"Could he tell you anything else?"

"Nope. But Mrs. Wandell, she had a few things to tell me."

"Mrs. who?"

"Wandell. She lives in the house across the street from the apartment. Nice lady. I met her coming along from the supermarket on Republican. She was having a time with her grocery bag." He frowned. "You'd think those clerks could use double bags when it's for an old lady even if she is only buying a couple a things. Bag was coming apart on her when I showed up."

I smiled to myself. Joey seems to have some kind of extrasensory affinity for older ladies. They not only like him, he likes them, and they talk to him, tell him things they wouldn't tell anyone else. He has a whole string of ladies in our neighborhood he runs errands for, sometimes gets their groceries, checks on to make sure they don't need anything.

"She's been living in that place for thirty years," Joey went on. "She knows all about everybody in the apartment. Everybody that's been there very long, anyway. Like Mr. Johnson. He lives in 107. He's been busted for speeding seventeen times. That's why he don't

drive anymore. They took his license away.
An' that lady, Ruby Chambers, she lives in the
apartment next to the nurse lady, she's been
arrested three times for shoplifting.'' He made
a wry face, shaking his head. ''She don't need
the stuff. She does it for fun. She feels sorry
for the nurse lady, Mrs. Wandell does. Says
she works too hard. Doesn't get home till the
middle of the night sometimes on Saturdays.''

''Where was she Friday night? Did she see
or hear anything? Mrs. Wandell, I mean.''

He sighed. ''Never heard a thing. She was
watching the tube and probably had it turned
up pretty loud. She don't hear too good. But
she did see something kinda interesting. She
didn't connect it to the dead guy, she didn't
even hear about him till the next day, but I
think it maybe might have something to do
with the murder. She saw someone walk out
the front door of the building just before eight-
thirty. Couldn't say who it was, not even if it
was a man or a woman, cause she wasn't paying that much attention, but she did see 'em.
Her front room window is right across from
the entrance. Whoever it was had on a hat and
pants and was kinda tall, which don't mean

much. Still, pretty strange anyone would leave with all the commotion going on.''

''Is she sure of the time?''

''Yep. She was waiting for her favorite program to come on at eight-thirty.''

I told him about the ten-thousand-dollar deposit of counterfeit bills.

He stared out the car window for a moment. ''That's not so good,'' he said finally. ''The guy she saw coulda been the one made the deposit. Or the killer. Means he does live in the place.'' He thought again. ''The kid at the Cornerpost said somebody passed two bad twenties in their place the same night Hiram was there. Wonder if there's a connection.''

I wondered, too.

When I got to the office I sat and spent some time deciding how I wanted to set up my database. As I saw it, I had two fields of inquiry. One, assessing Hiram's behavior patterns by documenting his past, the other, charting as much of his actual activities in the last six weeks as I knew about. The latter field could include negatives such as the fact that no one in the neighborhood had ever seen Hiram before I fell over him. The police had done a door-to-door inquiry, and yet it was there that he'd been found, dead.

Except the busboy. He was a real find. Whether the woman Hiram had been dining with was local or not, Hiram had been in the neighborhood, and it should be possible to find others who had seen him. The door-to-door Tom had ordered simply hadn't ranged far enough.

I booted up my big Pentium desktop unit and set to work. With even the best software, setting up a data management program takes a bit of time initially, but once you have it established, sorting, organizing, and correlating facts is a snap. When I stopped to get myself an apple for lunch, I printed out what I'd assembled so far and found I had twelve pages of information.

Bobby had assumed Hiram's identity in 1950, and although he had returned to his own name sometime prior to 1962, he had also used Hiram's identity right up to the day he died. He had registered at the Edgewater and rented the car as Hiram Taylor. The alias was his safety net. As Bobby, his only brushes with the law were the four complaints in Los Angeles during the sixties. As Hiram he had

never been convicted of anything but he'd
been implicated in a long list of offenses.

I stopped and thought. After so long was
there any way of sorting who did what? Hiram
or Bobby? We would have to find out for sure
what had happened to Hiram and if he was
still among the living. Or not.

I had found numerous complaints involving
women, one of which concerned a Denver socialite. Mrs. Ray Estes. The Denver paper had
faxed me a picture of her from their morgue.
It was hard to tell much from the grainy re-
production, but she appeared to be a good-
looking blond in her early fifties. Much the
same type of woman Bobby had been accused
of robbing in L.A.

Thinking about her led me to wondering
again about my neighbors. At least four
women in the building were tall, blue-eyed
blonds. None were the right age, but possibly
the age wasn't important. I hadn't given them
too much thought before, but the tenants were
certainly the logical suspects. If nothing else,
Hiram's body had been found on the premises.
The police had questioned everyone in the
building at least twice, and then again after
releasing Richard Bellam. They hadn't learned

anything significant, but that didn't mean there wasn't anything to learn. Of the blonds, both Edith and Sally Penny had been out of town, Inge had been upstairs in her own apartment before she came running to my rescue, but I didn't know about the fourth one, Katherine Davis.

By four o'clock I was starving so I shut everything down and walked over to my favorite restaurant, Julia's on 44th and Wallingford. Julia's is a small, offbeat kind of place with wonderful food. My favorite waitress, Dagmar, a perky little blond, told me the lemon piccata cod was especially good, so I ordered it and a pot of Chai tea.

I was halfway through my meal when I got a *huge* surprise. Sam walked in the door.

"Thought I might find you here," he said, brushing the top of my head with a kiss as he sat down. "Saw your car in the lot across the street."

I couldn't believe how glad I was to see him. I was even reckless enough to tell him so. "But what are you doing back so soon?" I asked. "Weren't you supposed to be in Virginia another week at least?"

"M-m-m-huh. I'll be going back tonight on

the red-eye. I've got a class at seven tomorrow morning. I'm cutting the course short, though. I'll be back again on Wednesday. Came back today to take a look at the Taylor case. Someone has to keep you out of trouble," he said, giving me a sardonic smile.

I opened my mouth to tell him I did not need him looking after me, but fortunately realized in time that he was putting me on. "I'm so glad, sir," I simpered. "Whatever would I do without you?"

"Not very well, from the sound of things," he said in a more sober voice. "I know there's no use telling you to stay out of things, Demary, but this is a nasty one and so far Neuman doesn't have any kind of a lead. Have you?"

For a moment I was surprised speechless. For Sam to ask me for a lead was not only a first, it was totally out of character.

"Neuman told you he didn't have a lead?" I asked, frowning. Something was out of kilter here. "He should have any number. I told him...Are you hungry? No? Let's get out of here, then. You can follow me over to the apartment where we can talk."

He agreed and a little later I was showing

him around the courtyard. He read the printouts I'd made earlier and asked the obvious
question. "Neuman has all of this?"

"Basically, yes. You can see what are facts
and what are my conclusions." I thought
surely he'd comment but he merely shrugged.

"Well, let's hope he's done more with it
than his last report suggests. I'm not going to
worry about it at the moment, anyway," he
said with a quick smile. "I've got more important things on my mind."

I had just realized that I hadn't told him
about the counterfeit money and didn't pick
up on his last remark for a moment. When
I did, I forgot the money. When he left at
eleven to catch his plane he still didn't know
about it.

TWELVE

I WAS DRINKING my first cup of coffee the next morning when Edith knocked on my door.

"For heaven's sake, why didn't you tell me about finding a body yesterday?" she asked as she came inside. Her hands fluttered about like butterflies, emphasizing her words. "I mean, tell me when I got back, not you found a body yesterday."

I laughed. Fractured English was Edith's trademark. "I guess it just didn't seem to be a good time. You were tired and I'd already given you a bad scare."

"It wasn't that bad. When Ruby Chambers started telling me about it this morning in the laundry room I thought she'd lost her mind, or been watching too much television. Was she right? Did you actually fall right on top of a dead man and get blood all over you?"

"Well, yes, I guess I did. Trip over him,

anyway. I didn't get all that much blood on me. Inge was the one who got blood all over her when she tried to take his pulse."

"Tell me about it." Edith plopped herself down on the couch.

Edith tickles me; somehow I couldn't believe she'd been the woman at the banking banquet. Or if she had been it was just the kind of nonsensical mistake she made all the time, not because of any interest she had in Gregory Holbrook. She's so alive, so interested in everything that happens around her, good, bad, or indifferent.

I told her the whole story, including most of what I had found out about Hiram. I was curious to know what her reactions would be. Her first remark was typical of her, a bit offbeat.

"What happened to his clothes? You can't tell a thing about a man if he's naked. You can't tell if he has any money, or education, or even good sense."

"Education? How can a man's clothes tell you about his education?"

"I've never seen a man with a decent education wearing blue jeans to the opera, or a tuxedo to a Sunday afternoon ball game."

I had to admit the truth of that. And also that as far as I knew none of his clothes had ever been found.

"Hmm. Strange," Edith commented. "Seems to me that would be the first order of business. Do you think the police have really looked? Or do you know where they looked?"

"I'm sure they've been trying to find them, but no, I don't know any details."

"You should find out. The clothes are important."

I didn't agree with her, or at least I didn't think finding his clothes would tell anyone much, nor did I think they would be found. Not in the sense of being identified as his, anyway. Clothes are too easy to get rid of. Washed and shorn of identification, they could have been dropped at any Salvation Army container, left in a Laundromat or in a downtown alley where someone would be sure to appropriate them.

Edith wouldn't give up on the clothes, though. She kept going back to them as long as we talked. She was determined there was great significance in Hiram being naked. I agreed that it had to do with identifying him, but I couldn't see that his undies would tell an investigator anything.

"Really, Demary," Edith said in an untypically dry tone. "Surely you've heard of DNA testing? Didn't you say he had a recent cut on his finger that had been stitched professionally? There's a record of that somewhere. And unless he was naked when he was killed there must have been blood on his clothes. Getting rid of blood-soaked clothes wouldn't be that simple, and keeping them, adding them to his own closet, would be even more dangerous. The clothes must have been distinctive in some other way, too. Identification. There's no other sensible reason for him being naked."

Edith is a great deal sharper than she appears.

I meant to ask her about the bank dinner, see what she'd say, but when my phone rang she waggled her fingers at me, said she'd see me later, and went out before I could stop her.

My friend Birdie Swallow was on the phone. She wanted to know if I'd bought our mutual friend, Katie Valentine, her birthday present. I'd talked to her weeks ago and had agreed to buy the present, plus mail it, which I'd done. Katie had married and moved to Del

Rio, New Mexico, several years ago. We both missed her. After thrashing out what she owed me we went on to some inconsequential chit-chat that ended with her asking me if I remembered a girl named Allison who had been in our sixth-grade class at Interlake School.

I dredged up a faint picture of a little towhead with big blue eyes and a terrific overbite. "I think so," I said, describing what I remembered of the girl.

"Yes, that's the one. Apparently she has a much better memory than either one of us. She recognized me immediately. I ran into her in the QFC supermarket yesterday and she reintroduced herself. She had read all about your murder in the paper."

"What do you mean, *my murder?*" I squawked. "*I* didn't kill the guy."

"Oh, you know what I mean."

"I'm tired of everybody calling it *my murder,*" I grumbled.

"Well, anyway, to get on with my story. Allison saw that man, Hiram, the weekend before he was killed."

"Where? Did she know him?"

"No, she didn't know him, and she isn't really positive, so she hasn't called the police.

But she's pretty sure it was him because she heard the woman call him Hiram and thought it was a funny old-fashioned name for such a hip-looking guy.''

"Where were they?''

"Having dinner at the Cornerpost.''

That fit with the busboy's account. "Did she describe the woman?''

"Some. She said she particularly noticed her because she was several inches taller than him. Hiram, I mean. She said she was a good-looking blond, quite a bit younger than he was, too.''

Hiram was certainly choosing the same type of woman right up to the end. "She needs to call the police.''

"I doubt if she does.''

"I'll tell Tom Neuman to call her, then. What's her married name?''

"I don't remember. I don't think she said.''

"Good grief, Birdie. Why didn't you ask?''

"Why in the world should I?'' Birdie replied indignantly. "I'm not a detective, and I haven't heard from you in a week. For all I knew you'd decided to take Katie's package to Del Rio yourself instead of mailing it.''

There was just enough truth in that to make

me feel guilty. I apologized and when we finally rang off we were back in good humor
with each other.

TOM CALLED late Sunday afternoon, said he
was in the neighborhood, and asked if I'd like
to have dinner at the Spaghetti Factory. He
spoke as if Friday's argument had never happened. Part of me wanted to tell him to stuff
it, but I couldn't make up my mind about him.
I couldn't understand why he'd done the report Sam had read without ever mentioning
some of the information I'd given him. Plus I
didn't know whether I liked him or whether I
couldn't stand him. Maybe another dinner
would set me straight. Besides which, I wanted
to know if he'd learned anything new.

He said he'd pick me up in an hour. I finished tidying up the kitchen, then went in to
take a shower.

Feeling perverse, and knowing that Tom
would probably be wearing jeans, I dressed in
an expensive haute-couture outfit of Sherry's
that I knew she didn't much like. It wasn't her
color. She'd been given it by a designer in
Italy. The dress hit her just below the knee but
came to my ankles and looked great on me. A

deceptively simple garment of pale sage-green cashmere, it slid over my head and settled on my hips like a second skin. With it I wore a short black caracul vest and a citron-yellow scarf.

For all the notice Tom took I might as well have been wearing a flour sack. He wasn't wearing jeans, however. He had on a pair of steel-blue wool slacks and a good-looking tweed jacket. While we were waiting to be seated I told him how nice he looked, but he seemed to be preoccupied and didn't respond in kind, which irritated me out of all proportion.

"Where have you been all dressed up?" I asked in an arch tone, still pursuing whatever it was I was on about.

"I was working. A homicide in that parking garage across from the opera house."

"What happened?" I asked, then wished I hadn't. I didn't really want to know about another killing. Especially not one that had taken place just three blocks from the Rosario.

"Looks like a mugging that went wrong. His wallet, watch, and ring are missing. He'd apparently been wearing the ring so long the perp had to rip considerable skin getting it off his finger. The body was found in the stairwell and as near as we can tell at the moment he was hit from behind with the traditional blunt instrument.''

''And he was probably on his way to church,'' I said bitterly.

''Not unless he was going to midnight Mass. Happened sometime last night. I have an idea…'' He stopped in mid-sentence as the hostess arrived and told us she had room in the bar.

''Have you talked to Edith since we walked in on her?'' he asked after we'd been seated and he had ordered wine for himself and tonic water with lime for me. ''Is she all right?''

''Sure. She's fine. I saw her this morning.''

''Where did she go on her vacation?''

''I don't know. She didn't say.'' Now that he mentioned it, I wondered why she hadn't said something.

''What did you talk about?''

''She wanted to know about the murder. Why?'' Tom could make the most casual question sound like he was interrogating an ax murderer.

''No reason. Did you tell her what you'd dug up on Hiram's past?''

"No, of course not," I lied, trying not to snap at him, and realizing at the same time that I should never have come. It's so seldom I carry a grudge I don't recognize the symptoms when I have them. "I haven't told anyone except you and Martha," I said, lying some more. "I am a licensed private investigator, you know, even if I don't work at it. George did teach me the basics. I don't go around blabbing about what I'm doing."

"Blabbing?"

"Talking. What is it that's bothering you about Edith, anyway?"

"Nothing. I was just curious where she'd been."

I was, too, now, but I wasn't going to tell him so. I made a mental note to ask her, though.

The conversation limped along for another few minutes and then our table was ready and we went in to dinner.

"What have you dug up this last couple of days?" Tom asked after we'd given our order to the college boy in ragged cutoff jeans who was masquerading as our waiter.

"I haven't been doing any digging. I've been trying to sort out what I already have.

But I did turn up another tall, blond woman. A Mrs. Estes, a socialite in Denver. She filed a complaint naming Hiram just last year. He apparently took her for a sizable chunk of cash, although the total wasn't given and the charges were dropped for lack of evidence, as usual.''

"Why are you wasting your time checking on these women? They don't have anything to do with his murder. Thousands of women fit the description. Your friend Edith does.''

"How do you know they don't? How do you know his killer isn't a woman?'' I demanded, beginning to get really annoyed. He had asked what I was doing. I hadn't volunteered.

"Don't be stupid. A woman didn't strip him and carry him out there on the porch. Where did you get such a dumb idea?''

"What's so dumb about it?'' Actually I hadn't thought about it at all, but it still wasn't a dumb idea. "How can you be so sure it wasn't a woman?''

"Because there isn't a sign of the body being dragged. Not in the hall or on the porch. No blood anywhere. Don't you think we know our job? We checked it out. Thoroughly.''

"Did you consider the possibility that she carried him?"

"Carried him? Now you are being ridiculous."

I started to shake. "The man weighed one hundred and sixty-five pounds. There are plenty of women who can carry that, and more."

"Maybe. But carrying him isn't the whole story. This was a violent crime. His whole head was smashed. It wasn't a woman's type crime."

"What was Lizzie Borden?"

"Okay, it happens, but women don't usually commit this kind of murder."

"Well, I commend your gallantry even if I can't commend your good sense," I said sarcastically.

He laughed. "Oh, come off it, Demary. You're just sore because I don't agree with you. Relax, tell me what else you've come up with."

Our waiter deposited salad plates in front of us and asked if we'd like fresh ground pepper. Tom said yes and chatted with the kid as he sprinkled it around. I sat there with my jaw sagging. Figuratively speaking.

It had finally seeped into my head that Tom had asked me to dinner with the sole purpose of learning what, if anything, I'd learned since we spoke last. And there was a strong possibility that information was the only reason he'd asked me out the first time.

I thought of tipping my salad in his lap, ground pepper and all, but managed to swallow the idea. Excusing myself, I got up quietly, picked up my bag, and walked out.

Fortunately there was a cab at the door depositing more diners. I'd forgotten I didn't have my own car.

The phone rang a few minutes after I got back to the apartment. It was Tom. I hung up as soon as I heard his voice, wondering how long it had taken him to realize I hadn't gone to the ladies' room.

I was still simmering when I got into bed. Then, minutes later, I remembered why I'd accepted his dinner invitation to start with. Talk about the pot calling the kettle black. I wasn't one bit better than he was.

I had a hard time getting to sleep.

THIRTEEN

MONDAY MORNING was hectic. I still hadn't caught up at noon when Jodie came in and asked if I wanted to go to lunch. I was too far behind to do so but I'm not sure I would have said yes in any case. She had on one of the most terrific outfits I'd ever seen. The competition would have been horrendous.

Her suit, a violet Ultrasuede that fit like it had been painted on her, was buttoned at the waist. With it she wore a deep purple blouse that cascaded out of the jacket's opening in multi-layered silk ruffles. The skirt was just above her knees, showing off her legs in pale violet-tinted hose.

"I just can't spare the time," I told her, admiring the suit. "One of my attorney clients goes to court tomorrow morning and I still haven't found all the precedent documentation he wants." I grinned at her. "Besides, I don't want to go anywhere with you when you're wearing that outfit.''

"Isn't it gorgeous? My sister gave it to me. She bought it for herself but her husband says it makes her look fat so she won't wear it. Personally, I wouldn't care what he said, I'd wear it anyway.''

I laughed. "Which is probably why you're still enjoying nonwedded bliss and she's married.''

"To a jerk. But anyway, what do you think of ol' Hiram's car being found that way? The rental one.''

"What? Found what way? Where, and when?''

"Neuman himself found it. Yesterday, Sunday morning. Didn't he tell you?''

"No, he didn't! Darn him, anyway.'' After thinking about my own motives I'd more or less gotten over being angry at him, but now I was mad all over again. There was no reason he couldn't have told me. In fact, the omission had to be deliberate; he had told me he'd been investigating a murder in the garage.

"Actually, Neuman didn't find it himself, but it was the same as. He was there at the time investigating another murder. Charles

McKensie, you know, the drama critic. He was killed Saturday night in the parking garage across from the opera house. They found his body yesterday morning. It must have happened late Saturday night after he left the performance of the *Barber of Seville*. At any rate, while the cops were looking around the garage because of McKensie, one of the brighter boys in blue spotted the license plate.''

''What a scuzzball that Tom is,'' I said angrily. ''He told me about McKensie's murder but never mentioned the car at all.''

''Well, he probably is a world-class jerk all right, but maybe he didn't think it was important.''

''How could he think it wasn't important? And how did you find out about it?''

''That pal of Dad's is in the motor vehicle department. The one he plays poker with. He told Dad about it after church yesterday. Tom may not have thought much of it because the car was all they found. There was nothing in it that belonged to Hiram. Nothing in the car, period.''

''How about fingerprints?''

''He didn't say, but there must have been plenty of them. It's a rented car, so there wouldn't be much way of telling which, if any, of the prints have anything to do with Hiram." She glanced at her watch. "I've gotta go. If I get a chance I'll call Dad's pal this afternoon and see if they've found out anything else."

"Aren't you pushing it a little, Jodie?" I asked. Jodie could play the well-bred junior miss when she wanted to, but she had all the finesse of a tank when it came to badgering a friend for something.

"Pushing what? Don't be silly. Anyway, what's to hide? He wouldn't know anything the cops wanted to keep quiet."

My phone rang as she waved at me and left.

It was Virginia Martineau. "I've changed my mind about the genealogy," she said without preamble. "Just send me your bill to date and drop the whole thing."

"All right," I said, as pleasantly as possible. I'd put a lot of time in on the darn search, and in fact, had only that morning sent for some new documents. However, it was her money. "Would you like me to send you what I've done?"

"Yes, I want all of it," she snapped, and hung up. Just like that, bang!

I sat for a moment with the phone still at

my ear, too surprised to react. Of all the rude things to do, hanging up on someone like that takes the prize in my book. It was odd behavior for her; she had always been extremely gracious. There was no point in worrying about it, though. I wasn't in any desperate need of clients, but it did seem strange.

An hour later Agent McBride came in and asked if I could spare him a few minutes. "I know you're busy, Ms. Jones, I talked to Martha on my way in, and I won't take long." He smiled. "I don't dare. Martha threatened me with a number of dire happenings if I took up too much of your time."

"Sure. Sit down. What can I do for you?" I asked, surprised by his diffident attitude. He was as big as ever, though, and I found him easier to take in a sitting position. He wasn't small even then. He looked particularly massive that day wearing an outrageous green tartan suit. I was beginning to suspect his choice of wearing apparel was deliberate. With your mind on his size and appearance you tended to forget about his being a government agent.

"Have you found out who deposited the money?" I asked.

"Not yet. What we have is more money."

"In my account? No, you can't have!"

"No, not in your account," he reassured me. "Most of it turned up in a routine count. The teller spotted it when she was balancing her cash after closing hours, so she doesn't know where it came from. I also learned about four other bills that were in a business deposit. In neither case were we able to trace the money back to the source, though."

"Couldn't the business people remember who'd given them the bills? Surely they'd take a good look at a bill that size. What kind of a business was it?"

"A restaurant. The one with the green striped awning that's a couple of blocks down from your apartment. The Cornerpost, I think it's called. Nobody paid any attention to these bills because they are only twenties. Very good twenties. The plates were done by the same hand as the hundreds but they aren't in the same class at all. The restaurant's bookkeeper says the deposit was made up on a Saturday night after a particularly busy day when none of the employees would have had time to do more than check the denomination of the money handed to them."

"Yes, I see. But how can I help you?"

"I'm not sure you can, or will even want to, but I'd like to ask. Martha tells me you really are a detective, as well as a researcher, so I'm hoping you can help me with this. I will, of course, pay your fees."

"Martha talks too much, and I'm not much of a detective. Besides, doesn't the Treasury Department have their own investigators? Why hire me? What are you looking for?"

"Yes, we do have our own, but I'd like to keep this confidential."

I couldn't be sure—Agent McBride's skin was very dark—but I was almost sure he was blushing. It made him seem a lot less government agent and a lot more human.

"Well, that's my business, confidential investigations," I said, grinning at him.

He smiled back. He did have a nice smile. "I'm probably doing this badly," he said ruefully. "My wife says I'm not good with words and I believe she's right, nonetheless…What I have in mind isn't complicated; I just don't want to suggest it to my superiors with nothing more to go on than a hunch. You see, I think now that the counterfeit money is connected to the dead man in your backyard, but, as I'm definitely not that kind of investigator, I have no way of substantiating my theory without admitting what I have in mind.''

''I don't understand. Don't the police, particularly the homicide department, know about the money?'' I asked, remembering that I hadn't talked to Sam about it, and as far as I could recollect hadn't mentioned it to Tom either.

''Not that I'm aware of. We don't keep the local police informed of what we're doing unless we have some reason to think they have information we can use. In this case there is no hard evidence that I know of. As I said, it's simply a hunch on my part.''

I told him it was an interesting idea and that I'd try to find something for him to hang it on, provided he'd do something for me. I wanted him to look for some information I didn't have access to. He said he'd try. We agreed on a trade, and he left, promising he'd get back to me soon. What I didn't tell him was that I had already come to the same conclusion about the money and the murder that he had. When I'm being confidential I go all the way.

So far, all the counterfeit money had been found in the local branch bank, which to me suggested that either the counterfeiter was local, or that the money was held locally. Given that idea, Hiram was an obvious possibility. Plus Hiram had dinner at the Cornerpost and the busboy said someone had given them counterfeit money that night. Probably the same bills Sean was talking about. What I didn't understand was why more twenty-dollar bills hadn't turned up. I was beginning to have an idea about the money deposited to my account, but the other money baffled me.

Bobby's use of Hiram's name made me certain he had come to Seattle for a scam of some kind and it could easily have been something to do with counterfeit money. In one of the complaints filed against him the woman involved said the bundle of money Hiram had shown her to prove his honesty had looked ''funny'' but of course she didn't have a sample.

I went through the file printouts I'd taken home, then plugged my computer into one of the national databases and started prowling through its records looking for the names of my apartment neighbors. I'd been meaning to do that for several days but kept forgetting. Not that I had any specific reason to think one of them might be guilty, but they were all suspects.

I switched databases a couple of times, finding some names in rather odd places. Inge, for instance, was on quite a few lists as a registered nurse, but I also found her named as the complainant in a malpractice suit tried four years ago in Wyoming. That surprised me.

Richard Bellam's record showed several aliases, including Bellingham, which I found curious.

I was about to switch to another database, since I wasn't turning up anything relevant in the one I was on, when I stumbled onto a real shocker. An arrest record on Edith Myrdice Vibike for carrying a concealed weapon without a license. The spelling of Edith's name is so unusual it leapt off the screen at me.

It was recent, in fact only two months ago, originating out of the Portland, Oregon, airport. It wasn't a regular police record; in fact, it wasn't an arrest record at all. It was an interoffice memo request made by airport security asking for information on a passport. The passport number was in code and I couldn't tell from the wording whether she had been leaving the country or entering it. There was nothing further.

When McBride called at 6:30 with the information I had asked for I was able to fill in another blank, but it didn't get me any closer to finding Hiram's killer. I'd been reasonably sure Bobby had only used Hiram's identity when he was short of cash, and sure enough, every time I could document Hiram, Bobby's bank balance was in sore need of a transfusion.

I told McBride how I was doing, then said I had another request. I wanted a copy of Edith's bankcard charges for the past month.

"That's a bit touchy," McBride said thoughtfully. "I'm not sure I can show cause."

"Do you have to? I mean, as a Treasury Agent you do have access to bank records."

"Not without a warrant. And charge cards, MasterCard and so forth, are quite a different thing. However, I'll try. If I can't get a hard copy without tipping our hand..." He interrupted himself to chuckle. "What shall I look for?"

"Check where she's made charges in the last couple of weeks. She may have paid cash, but take a look anyway. Especially the week-end after the murder.''

''I'll see what I can do. Anything else?''

''Yes.'' I gave him three more names and asked him to check their bank records for source of income. ''These are all legitimate inquiries. I mean you can show good cause on these. All of these people live in the apart-ment. They all have some kind of a criminal record—however minor—so are possibilities as far as having been in possession of coun-terfeit money. Or of having deposited the stuff in my account. Anyone of them might have found one of my deposit slips in the trash.''

''Is there a possibility one of them is guilty of murder?''

''They all had opportunity, and no alibi. Motive—maybe, maybe not. In this case I think we have to work backward anyway.''

''Backward?''

''Yes. I think we have to find our suspect first, and then look for the motive. Usually it's the other way around, but Bobby was such a rotter almost anyone might have had reason to clobber him.''

''Ms. Jones—''

''Mr. McBride, would you mind calling me

Demary?'' I interrupted. ''I find that Ms. business awkward.''

''Demary, then. And you will please call me
Sean?''

A small laugh escaped me. ''I'm sorry,
Sean,'' I apologized. ''The name just doesn't
seem to fit you.''

''I know.'' He sighed theatrically. ''My
mother was addicted to Irish poetry, and with
the name McBride she simply couldn't help
herself, I guess. My sisters' names are Fiona
and Cathleen.''

That tickled me.

''So, where were we? Ah, yes, I was about
to ask how much of your information is known
to the local police.''

''I have no idea now. Certainly I've not
given them any lately,'' I said, not adding that
I was through giving one member of the local
homicide squad as the time of day, let alone
anything concerning Hiram.

''I'm not sure that's wise. I'm quite used to
working without any local police support.
There usually isn't any reason for it. But in
this case...'' His voice trailed off question-
ingly.

''You're right, of course. We will have to

turn it over to them, if and when we have anything solid, but at the moment all we have is
a lot of guesses, and a hunch. Which reminds
me, you said you had a hunch the two cases
were related but you didn't say what gave you
the idea. Mind telling me?''

He hesitated, then said, "No, not at all. It's
just such a small thing I'm not sure...
However, last year in Denver I worked on a
case where I encountered twenties that I'm
sure were made with the same plates as these
here in Seattle. And while I was there I heard
about a confidence trickster who was operating
in the area. His description matches that of
your dead man, but I never heard his name.''

"When? When was it?'' I asked, scrabbling
through the papers on my desk, trying to find
the one about the Denver socialite. "Was it
last spring?''

"Yes, in May.''

"Bingo! We've got a connection.'' I was so
excited I jumped to my feet and knocked my
chair flying. "The Denver cops brought
Bobby, or Hiram, whichever you want to call
him, in for questioning on May 17. It doesn't
prove anything, but it's one heck of a possibility.''

FOURTEEN

I WENT TO WORK Tuesday morning feeling ten feet tall. Tying Hiram—possibly—to the counterfeit money had been a major breakthrough. We didn't have any hard evidence, and on the surface it didn't get us any closer to his killer, or prove anything at all for that matter, but what we had was enough for me. It filled in some blanks and it was quite a coup for Agent McBride. He planned on seeing his superior first thing that morning, and although he didn't know where the Treasury Department might take it from there, he promised to get me the information I wanted whatever the brass decided to do.

I was beginning to have an idea what happened that Friday and I was hoping McBride could get me some confirmation. I certainly didn't plan on asking Tom Neuman for any help. Every time I even thought of the man I could feel my blood pressure going up.

Carol Ann called shortly after I got to the office.

"Hey, kid, guess what?" she greeted me. "I finally got around to calling Charlie again and what do you know, Neuman is married. Hope you weren't planning on any wedding bells soon yourself."

I simply gasped. Carol Ann laughed and hung up.

For a moment I wasn't even angry. I was stunned. Not that there was, or had been, anything like a romance between us, in fact pretty much the opposite, but what the heck was he doing asking another woman out to dinner if he was married?

"He was fishing for information, just like you thought, you dumbbell," I muttered. That struck me so funny I laughed aloud.

"What's so funny?" Martha asked, coming to the door.

I told her.

"The cheek of him," she said, grinning. "Teach you you're no femme fatale anyway."

"It should teach me something," I agreed. "Don't run off," I said as she deposited the mail on my desk and turned to go. "I'd like to know something about your friend Sean."

She frowned. "Know what? It's his wife Rene I went to school with."

"Yes, I know that, but I'm curious about his job. What did you mean when you said he was tracing Holocaust gold?"

"Oh. Well, I'm not sure you'd have paid any attention, although it does tie in with the Holbrik case, but Congress unanimously adopted, and Clinton signed, the War Crimes Disclosure Act in 1996, which more or less forced the Swiss to change their policy regarding the money belonging to Holocaust survivors and their heirs."

I nodded. As I mentioned previously, I'd actually been very interested in the law. The purpose of the act was to enable Holocaust survivors and/or their descendants to claim the gold the Nazis stole from them and deposited in Swiss banks. Banks secrecy, however, is Switzerland's most sacrosanct law. A law passed in the early 1930s, if I remembered the date correctly, made it a jail offense for anyone in the banking business to even talk to their wives about bank business. Swiss banks can and do refuse to give out any kind of information, let alone release any monies, without account numbers or absolute proof of ownership, such as death certificates. Which in the past has made it extremely difficult for survivor families, as the death camp authorities didn't bother with such niceties.

"I know about the problems, but where does Sean come into the story?" I asked.

"Sean is an expert, and I do mean an expert, at following money. His normal job is tracing mob money. How they launder it, tracing their triangular transactions, which, according to Rene, is what the Germans did with the money they looted from occupied countries."

"Triangular transactions?"

She nodded. "The way the Germans did it, they delivered stolen or what you might call suspect money and/or gold to the Swiss banks in exchange for Swiss francs. That much of the transaction involved the actual money or gold; everything else was on paper. Once they had the credit in Swiss francs the Germans could purchase raw materials from so-called neutral countries, as francs were accepted everywhere. Then the neutral banks could purchase gold from the Swiss banks with these same francs. Get it? Round and round we go?''

I nodded.

''Well, mob money-men do much the same thing. Anyway, earlier this year there was a big hoo-haw when a number of ultrasecret Nazi files concerning Jewish gold disappeared. The gold, stolen from Jews sent to the camps, was supposedly delivered to Berlin and then routed on to Swiss banks. The amount was probably close to a billion dollars at today's prices. There is no record of what happened to it after it arrived in Berlin, but in the remaining files there was a hint that part of the gold was rerouted, possibly to Brazil and later to Hong Kong.''

''And that's what Sean is trying to prove, or follow?''

''Yes, but not alone. That's what his department's been doing for quite some time but recently they have found traces of someone else doing the same thing. Someone based, they think, in Seattle. So that's why he's here, to see if he can winkle out who it is. Normally he works out of San Francisco. And incidentally, that information is not for public consumption. I got most of it from Rene. He doesn't talk about what he does.''

"Sounds very James Bond.''

"Sean? Not likely. Sean's about as unobtrusive as a concrete truck. And anyway, he works electronically most of the time.''

"So tracing the counterfeit bills deposited to my account is just a sidebar?''

"Yes. I think so. Either that or he may think it's mob connected.''

THE MAN HIMSELF called shortly before noon. He had all the income sources I wanted, plus information on Edith.

"There are no charges on her bankcard for five days before the murder and only one charge since,'' he told me. "She checked into the Golden Lion Motel in Portland on Friday, or actually on Saturday, as she didn't arrive until three in the morning. She checked out last Friday. No other charges. Does that help you?''

"I'm not sure. I'll have to think about it. Did you check the source of her income?''

"As far as I could tell in the time I had, the bulk of her income is from a single electronic

deposit made once a month. Very difficult to
trace. She carries a seven-figure balance.''

I blinked. That was one heck of a lot of
money for a checking account balance.
''Thanks, Sean. How'd it go with your boss
this morning?''

''Not as well as I'd hoped. I don't believe
the man was too pleased with me. I got the
distinct feeling he thinks I should have kept
my nose to the counterfeit grindstone and not
been worrying about a murder. However, if
the dead man proves to have been responsible
for the counterfeit he may change his mind. I
guess *proof* is the operative word here.''

''It always is,'' I told him cheerfully.

I worked fairly steadily for the rest of the
day. I finished a rather tricky job for one of
my insurance company clients and was gath-
ering Virginia Martineau's material together,
getting it ready to mail to her, when I spotted
the information she was undoubtedly trying to
hide. It was there in the birth certificate copies
I'd received in the mail that morning. One of
the spelling name-changes had been done by
Virginia's great-grandfather. And if I had the
connection straight, that same man was Ri-

chard Bellam's great-grandfather's brother.
Which made them second or third cousins.

No wonder Bellam had been released from
police custody so quickly. Her husband would
have seen to that in a hurry. With elections
less than a year away he wouldn't want a family scandal to surface, no matter how remote
the connection. In fact, Virginia might have
been the woman Bellam was with at the
Edgewater.

I put everything in a big manila envelope
and was ready to give it to Martha to type up
the bill when it occurred to me that there might
be another connection. I hadn't thought of it
before because she had no obvious connection
to Hiram, but Virginia too was tall, blond,
blue-eyed, and close to the right age. Had Virginia been one of Hiram's victims? She didn't
fit my profile of the killer, but that didn't mean
she couldn't be involved. Had I figured it all
wrong?

I called to Martha to come get the envelope
and told her I wanted to run an idea past her.

"What idea?" she asked, twitching at the
mariner's compass wall hanging as she came
in. I guessed I was going to have to go back

to the flame-colored one before she twitched
the poor thing totally out of shape.

I told her about Virginia's connection to
Bellam and the possibility that she might have
known Hiram, but she shook her head.

"If you're thinking she might have offed
him herself, you can forget it," she said.
"There was a big political dinner in Olympia
that night. She and the senator were there. I
saw pictures of them with the governor in the
Sunday paper."

"Well, I didn't think she did it herself, but
she could have hired sodeone."

"You've been reading too many cheap novels," she said, shooting me a dour look as she
went back to her own desk. The fax machine
was clattering out what sounded like a lengthy
message.

She came back a minute later waving a
sheaf of papers.

"Got him," she said triumphantly. "Grogory Holbrik had his name changed to Gregory
Holbrook by Poll something, legal anyway, on
June 25, 1997, in a Hong Kong court, one
week before the Chinese took over. He probably figured with so much else going on

his little pack of lies would get lost in the shuffle.''

"What else? It looks like you have his life history there.''

"I practically do! One of my computer pals got onto someone she knew in Hong Kong and got me all this stuff.''

Over the past few years Martha has built up what amounts to a personal network of computer informants all over the country that she talks to via chat rooms, e-mail, and bulletin boards. They not only exchange all kinds of information, some of her correspondents seem to get a big kick out of digging for the information she wants through the back issues of their local newspapers, government records, plain old gossip, and anything else they can think of. The fax Martha handed me appeared to be legal records.

Grogory Holbrik had indeed had his name legally changed and in the course of doing so had supplied the court with considerable information. Part of which looked suspiciously like a load of plum duff, according to Martha.

"Look here,'' she said, pointing with a slim finger. "Says here he was born in July 1961, in São Paulo. Mother Johana Holbrik, father

Grogory Maarten Holbrik. Grogory Maarten had already been dead well over a year by that time. Now either that was the longest pregnancy on record or somebody got their story wrong.''

I scanned several more pages. "I think we have Mr. Holbrook by the nose," I said, grinning. "Or Jan and family do. Is Anna around? I think she'd better be the one to take over from here and I'd like to talk to her before I call Jan."

"No, she's in court today, but Jodie is in. I'll tell her to set up a meeting with Anna for tomorrow sometime. Okay?"

I nodded. "In the meantime, thinking of all your computer pals, do you have one in Portland?"

"M-m-huh. Two in fact."

"Get on to them, will you, and see if they can find out what Edith was doing in Portland for a week."

She nodded. "I'll try, but Portland's a big city. Not likely she did anything to bring attention to herself."

"No, but I have a feeling... She stayed at the Golden Lion; they might pick up something there.'' I thought for a moment, remembering that weird interoffice memo about Edith. ''Tell them to try the airport, too. International flights especially.''

FIFTEEN

IT WAS POURING DOWN rain when I woke the next morning. The last of the fall flowers in the beds around the courtyard were pounded flat into the mud. I was late, I'd forgotten to set my alarm, so I skipped breakfast, pulled on a pair of Dockers and a heavy cable-knit sweater, and headed for the office. I had an idea I wanted to get started on, plus I wanted to check the progress on my house.

A mistake on my part not taking the time for coffee. I had a screaming headache and was in a seriously bad mood—no one was working on my house—by the time I unlocked my door. Martha was late, too.

In fact, I discovered there was no one in the building at all when I went stomping down the hall to Anna's. I was ready to have her do something drastic about the contractor, so it was just as well she wasn't there. My head-

ache disappeared and I was in a more reasonable frame of mind after two cups of coffee.
The carpenters would have had a difficult time
of it trying to work on the porch in what was
turning out to be a real humdinger of a storm.
Not only was the rain coming down in buck-
ets, the wind was snapping tree branches and
sending debris slamming against the outside
walls.

My own office doesn't have windows and
so I had that snug feeling, safe from the ele-
ments, when I booted up my computer and
went to work. While I was in the shower I'd
had a thought that I should have had sometime
before.

I'd assumed from the beginning, reinforced
by Tom Neuman pooh-poohing the idea, that
Hiram's killer was a woman. There was no
evidence of that at all. In fact, as Tom had
insisted, it really wasn't a typical woman's
crime. For one thing, for a woman to approach
him with a weapon that could bash his head
in without alerting him was stretching believ-
ability. Neither his hands nor his arms had
shown any sign of bruising, of trying to protect himself, or of being tied. He could have
been in bed, or taking a shower, which might

account for his lack of clothes, but it was equally possible that his killer had been a man. Just because the only documented evidence against Hiram I'd found were scams involving women, did not mean they were the only crimes he'd committed.

What I needed to do now was to look for any involvement Hiram had with a man, either as the victim of one of his scams, or, and this was possibly a better idea, as his partner in something illegal. Possibly, and this was a new idea, with his brother. I didn't bother looking for anything legal—I doubted if he had a legal bone in his body—but the first thing I found was that Hiram, as Bobby, had a perfectly legitimate job as a used car salesman in Eureka, California. The owner of the place had a pretty shaky background, in fact he had a decidedly murky past, but Hiram/Bobby's record in Eureka seemed to be soap-bubble clean.

I prowled through every source I could access and as soon as Martha came in I told her to get on the Internet and see what she could find out from her computer pals. Some of her correspondents are willing to drop anything they are doing to look for what she wants. They seem to get a big charge out of doing it.

Most of them are good at it, too, and they all seem to be particularly good at garnering plain old back-fence gossip.

Back-fence gossip, always the most reliable, paid off before noon.

First, though, was a call from Joey, apparently between classes, on his recently acquired cell phone. I could hear a bedlam of young voices in the background as he spoke. "Demary, you need to get pictures of all the blond ladies got anything to do with this case," he said hurriedly. "Ho saw the one Hiram was with on the street, but he don't know her name. He tried to follow her but she spotted him and scared him off. I ain't had time to scope out all the poop. I'll get back to you." I heard a bell in the background as he hung up.

"What was that about?" Martha asked. We'd been talking when the phone rang. "Your mouth is hanging open."

"That darn Joey." I told her what he'd said. "Now where in the heck does he think I can get their pictures? And I wish he'd stay out of this. I'm always afraid he'll ask questions in the wrong place. Of the wrong person. Or get one of his little friends in trouble."

"Sounds like he was in school. Not too many villains around there."

"Don't kid yourself. They get younger every day."

"I wonder if his mother doesn't get upset the way he goes tearing off after you sometimes."

"Yes, but she says it doesn't bother her because she always knows where he is. In fact, I got the distinct impression that he tells her exactly what he's doing and why, and that she gets a kick out of it."

"When did you talk to her?" Martha asked, surprised.

"It was quite a while ago now. When we were trying to solve the Electric Toy thing. I met her in QFC. Actually, I thought she was going to tell me to stay away from Joey and I was wondering how I could tell her there was no way I could force Joey into doing, or not doing, anything. He does his own thing." I chuckled, remembering. "And that was practically the first thing she said to me. That I wasn't to feel responsible for Joey, that he goes his own way regardless."

I could hear her soft voice in memory. *"Joe and I raised Joey to be independent and strong-minded, and although we always want to know what he's doing, he knows he is the only one accountable for his actions. Providing, of course, that he doesn't do something we have prohibited. It seemed like a good idea at the time but it has rather backfired on us,"* she'd said, smiling in her vague way. *"He's a bit too independent at times, but he is good about keeping in touch, especially when Joe is away, and more than good now that he has the cell phone and pager. To tell the truth, I sometimes wonder if he isn't keeping track of me rather than the other way around."*

I smiled, thinking about him. Joey was definitely his own man. "Anyway, what were you starting to say when the phone rang?" I asked.

She handed me several pages of the fax. "Got this from a mate in Denver. She sent the newspaper stuff with her scanner, but the real story is what she heard from her sister's next-door neighbor. You knew about the Denver cops hauling Hiram in last May?" I nodded. "They had to let him go when the lady refused to press charges, that was in the paper, but what the newshounds didn't get a handle on was that her husband, Ray Estes, took a shot at Hiram later that same day.''

''You're kidding me! And the papers never heard about it?''

''They may have heard, but the story never hit the street. The lady's husband is old-line Denver. His family helped settle the town. No doubt he owns the right people; what he doesn't own is his next-door neighbor who doesn't happen to like him. She told her sister and she... Never mind all that. What happened was, Ray figured Hiram had a bit more to do with the lady than just taking her for a wad of lolly. So Hiram, not being slow in the head, took off for the airport the minute he was released from the nick. Unfortunately for Hiram, Ray isn't slow, either. He figured Hiram would make a run for it and was waiting for him at the terminal where he cornered him on one of those transports they have to take you back and forth from the boarding areas.''

I goggled at her. ''You mean he shot Hiram right out in front of everybody?''

''Not quite. I said he wasn't stupid. He stuck a gun in Hiram's ribs and marched him off down some back stairs where he undoubtedly intended to do Hiram some major damage. Somewhere en route, though, Hiram managed to give him the slip and took off running, whereupon Ray lost his cool and took three shots at him. There were a number of people around at the time, maintenance and airport personnel, one of whom tackled Ray and took his gun away. They expected Hiram to raise all kinds of fuss, but by the time they had Ray under control Hiram had disappeared into the gloaming, so to speak. Needless to say, he didn't report the incident to anyone. Nor did he use his plane ticket. How he got out of Denver isn't known. At least not by my informant's sister's neighbor.''

''So the whole thing just got shoved under the rug?''

''Well, not quite. Ray was arrested, charged with reckless endangerment, carrying a concealed weapon without a license, and a half dozen other things too, but with no Hiram to bring charges and no one actually hurt, the judge apparently decided the incident wasn't worth more than a fine and a suspended sentence.

''Jeeze.''

''And that's only the half of it.''

''There's more?''

"Oh, yes. It does get better." Martha rolled her eyes. "Guess where Ray was the night Hiram got it?"

"Not in Seattle?"

"Even better. Not only was Ray Estes in Seattle, he was staying at the Edgewater Hotel, and so was the beautiful Denver socialite Mrs. Ray Estes."

"Oh, my!"

"Right. And according to the maid who did their room he was 'out' all day and evening. She, Mrs. Estes, was 'in' part of the time. She was in the lobby, and then in the bar, from six o'clock until nearly eight, obviously waiting for someone and was overheard telling the bartender she was expecting her husband any minute. At about eight she got a phone call and then had the barman call her a cab and from then on I don't know."

"Where in the world did you get all that?"

She grinned. "Third hand, but I'll give you odds it's correct. The bell-man is dating the sister of a girl in one of my husband's classes. What I don't know is how they knew you'd be interested." She paused, thinking. "H-m-m. The girl knows I work for you, your name was in the paper the morning after the murder

along with all the rest of the story, the Edgewater was mentioned a couple of days later, as
was the story of the blond woman who met
with Bellam at the Edgewater. Mrs. Estes is
blond, and she was there the night Hiram got
it. Given the Byzantine thinking of some of
those kids at the U…Yes, that's why she called
me a few minutes ago.''

''Good grief. Your information network
puts the CIA to shame.''

Martha smirked, tossing her head. ''Don't
knock it, girl,'' she said, hips swinging as she
went back to her own desk to answer the
phone.

The caller was Anna Carmine. She wanted
me to bring all my information on Gregory
Holbrook, née Grogory Holbrik, down to her
office. Which I promptly did. Among other
things I always love to see what Anna is wearing. Five foot five, bony and angular—both in
figure and personality—Anna dresses in the
most interesting high-style clothes I've ever
seen. She wears her black hair in a feathered
cut somewhat like Liza Minnelli, and although
not at all beautiful she is very striking. Today
she had on a straight-cut black-and-brown
print dress that hung straight from her shoul-

ders to her toes and should have looked like a
nightgown; instead it looked terrific. It looked
like some kind of South American tribal cer-
emonial gown, complete with heavy gold
chains.

After reading what I had and talking for a
while she agreed to represent Jan and his parents if they wanted her.

"You call him and set up a meeting for Friday at two o'clock," she said, checking her
calendar. "And in the meantime I need more
information on the man."

"What kind?"

"Where he's living now, his job, if he has
one, married or not, and if so to whom and
how long, is he part of any class action suit
concerning the Swiss gold, and most important, does he go to synagogue."

I nodded. "Why synagogue?"

"If he is attending he will have had to give
them extensive information, which may or
may not be truthful, as I don't suppose they
would have checked, but I want to know if he
took the chance."

"You'll have it all by Friday morning, some
by tomorrow," I promised. This was the kind
of thing I'm good at and so is Martha. Martha

is a computer genius. Most of this kind of information is on a computer somewhere and if you are anywhere in a computer Martha can find you. Sometimes I think she must have computer chips implanted in that beautiful head of hers.

The phone was ringing when I got back to my own place. Martha handed it to me with what I can only describe as a smirk.

It was Sam. He was home. I was so glad to hear him I felt as giddy as a lovesick teenager. I agreed with almost indecent haste when he said he'd pick me up at seven and take me out to dinner.

SIXTEEN

JOEY CAME PELTING across the parking lot when I went out to get in the Toyota. He looked like a drowned cat, hair plastered to his skull with water dripping off the ends and down the neck of his open jacket.

"Good grief, Joey," I gasped. "You're going to catch your death of cold. Get in the car, I'll take you home."

"You don't necessarily catch cold from being wet," he informed me in a bookish tone as he settled himself in the passenger seat. "In fact, explorers who frequently spend days in wet clothes very seldom catch a cold at all. The infantry soldiers in World War II who slogged halfway across Europe chasing Hitler's army the winter of 1944/45 were wet and muddy for weeks at a time, but they didn't catch any more colds than the people here at home. They got more trench foot than anything else.''

I looked at him with surprised respect. Nineteen forty-four-forty-five was ancient history to him. "How do you know?" I asked.

"Read it in a medical journal," he said archly.

I grinned. Joey did love to catch me with stuff like that.

"I need those pictures," he said, switching subjects. "That blond who was with Hiram the night at the Cornerpost must be guilty of something or she woulda spoke up before now. I wanted to take Ho over to the apartment and stake it out, watch for the woman, but he won't do it. He's too scared. I think maybe his family is illegals."

"*No,*" I gasped. "Don't even think of doing that. She probably just doesn't want to get involved. You could get in all kinds of trouble."

"What trouble?" he asked, giving me a withering look. "Who's going to suspect anything of a couple a dumb kids tossing a ball around?"

"In the rain?"

"Yeah, that's a problem," he agreed, opening the door. I'd stopped in front of his house. "I'll think of something," he added, racing up the walkway for his door.

SHERRY WAS STANDING in the garage talking to Inge when I drove up the alley to the door. I was surprised to see her. I thought she was flying directly to a photo shoot in Mexico City from the one she'd been on in Milan.

"Hi, beautiful," I called, rolling my window down. "Welcome home. I'll go around and park in front."

"No, don't do that," she called back. The sound of the rain on the garage roof made hearing a normal voice impossible. "I'm leaving again in a couple of hours. Back up and give me some room. I'll go park around front."

I backed up a good long way. Sherry was a notoriously bad driver and the Toyota didn't need anymore dings than it already had. The motor was in perfect condition due to my friendly neighborhood mechanic, but it did look a bit banged up.

We met in the apartment a few minutes later.

Sherry is one of the nicest people I have

ever known, which in my experience is not always true of a female as beautiful as she is. When we were kids and all our friends started filling out in the right places, Sherry simply got taller and cried a lot. Then her mother sent her to a charm school and the rest was inescapable. She went to work for a local modeling company while she was still in high school and eventually became one of the top ten models in the country. She is five eleven, still has a figure like a yardstick, has wonderful cheekbones, dark brown hair that curves under at her shoulders, and photographs like a dream. The perfect model.

According to her, modeling is not particularly hard and can be incredibly boring. She claims she spends half her time in a hot, stuffy dressing room half naked while someone with ice-cold hands fits a garment on her.

I knew she was hoping to quit soon, so her first words as she flung her arms around me in a quick hug weren't a real shock.

"I'm through, Demary," she said, her eyes sparkling with joy. "This is my last job."

"I thought you were booked for a show in Mexico City."

"I am, I am. But that's the last one. I've

got my ranch. That's why I came home. To sign the papers. I told them I'd be a day late in Mexico. I didn't care if they liked it or not. I've got it! I've actually got my ranch, De-mary.''

She danced me around the room, laughing and so excited her whole face shone with delight. Sherry has been horse mad since she was not much more than a toddler, and has been saving her money for a small ranch from the time she earned her first dollar baby-sitting.

I was more than pleased for her and wanted to know all the details.

''You know I've had that real-estate agent friend of my mother's looking for a place for me for ages. Yes?''

I nodded, pulling my clothes off as she talked. Sam would be picking me up in just over an hour and I wanted plenty of time for a shower and some makeup. I wanted to look especially good.

''She found the perfect place a couple of months ago. I went with her to look and loved it. It's up near where your brother lives, just north of Startup. Off the road to Spada Lake.

It's perfect! Twenty-five acres, cross-fenced, and with a beautiful brick barn. I love it.''

"Does it have a house?" I asked, grinning at her.

"House? Oh, yes. Well, the house isn't much but that's all right. It's a perfect place to raise horses."

I couldn't help laughing. The house could be falling down and she wouldn't have cared as long as the barn was in good shape. "Well, how come you didn't sign immediately?" I asked.

"They wanted more than I could afford if I was going to have anything left over for a good stud. But they came down to my price yesterday," she said, practically yodeling with glee.

I left her still prancing around the room when I went to take my shower.

"Say, what's this Inge said about you finding a dead body?" she asked when I came back out and started pawing through the few clothes I had in the closet. I wanted something festive.

I told her, abbreviating the story as much as possible, and particularly not including any gory details.

Her face took on a slightly green tinge. "How perfectly horrible for you," she said, shuddering. "Awful. Makes me queasy just hearing about it secondhand. Lucky Inge was there to stand by. I've never cared much for her, she has always seemed so cold somehow, but I can see that it's probably just a professional façade."

"She was certainly a staunch ally that night. As you say, probably because she's a nurse and didn't want me keeling over or something," I said absently, pulling another dress out where I could see it.

"What are you looking for?" Sherry asked. "Where are you going?"

"Something to wear out to dinner with Sam. He just came back."

"Oh. Well, you need something special, then," she said, pushing me out of the way. She rummaged at the back of the closet for a moment, then handed me a pale pink wool dress that looked like it was made out of that cotton candy floss you see at the Puyallup Fair.

"Pink? With *my* hair?"

"It will look great on you. It's almost a mini on me but will hit you calf-length. Just right. Black high heels and a black patent belt.'' She pulled open a drawer in the dresser and handed out the approved belt. ''Now what about this body?''

Between getting dressed and putting on the small amount of makeup I'm capable of applying I told her most of what I knew about Hiram/Bobby.

''I think you need to get out of here and go stay with your mother and dad until they find the killer,'' she said bluntly when I finished. ''It's got to be someone here in the Rosario. You're the proverbial sitting duck living here.''

''Not necessarily,'' I protested. I explained about the gate behind the laundry room and the other entrances and how anyone could have gotten into the courtyard.

''That's crazy,'' she said sharply. ''Why in the world would anyone bring a dead body *into* the courtyard or the apartment? Doesn't make sense. There's no place around here to hide a body. What were they going to do with it, run it down the disposal? Whoever it was was trying to get the body out of the place. Not into it. What's got your thinking so muddled, Demary?''

Two hours later Sam said practically the same thing. In the same tone of voice.

"You're not safe in that place," he said. "Our killer is either living there or has ready access to the building. A relative, friend, ex-husband, something. I'd feel a lot better about it if you'd go stay with your folks."

I scowled. I'd gotten over being so scared and I hated having to move from one place to another. I wanted to go home. "You don't have any proof of that," I said finally. "That it's someone in the building."

"No, but if you'd use your head a little you know it has to be. No one in their right mind would be bringing a dead body into the building. He was getting it out. Or trying to."

"Well, why hasn't Neuman done—"

"Neuman is a perfectly competent investigator," he interrupted. "He's inexperienced, and maybe slow, but he hasn't mismanaged anything."

"Bull cookies," I said angrily. "Hiram was seen having dinner at the Cornerpost with a local woman the week before he was killed. She could very well be the killer. I knew that days ago and I don't think Neuman has discovered it yet. That's how darn competent he is!''

Sam's eyes narrowed to angry slits. "Did you tell him?''

"No! Why should I do his blasted work for him?''

"How do you know she was local? And just what else do you know that you haven't reported?'' he demanded.

"I know darn well he hasn't had the neighborhood canvassed the way he should. He hasn't done half enough checking on the tenants. He hasn't even discovered that Hiram was passing counterfeit.'' That last was pure guesswork but I knew it was true. Hiram had something to do with the stuff and Tom Neuman should have gotten onto it days ago. He should have gotten onto the Estes setup, too. The police had ten times as much investigative power as I did. There was no darn excuse for the way Neuman was handling this case and I said so.

"Then you had better set me straight,'' Sam snapped, angry. "Just exactly what have you dug up that proves you're such a much better investigator than the Seattle Homicide Department?''

I had such a sudden overwhelming sense of déjà vu I nearly blanked out. We weren't at the Spaghetti Factory but otherwise the scene was exactly the same as the one I'd gone through with Tom Neuman the previous Friday.

And I reacted the same.

"Excuse me," I said abruptly and headed for the ladies' room. Out of Sam's sight I made a sharp left turn, caught a cab outside the building, and went home. I was so mad I felt sick. Sam had invited me to dinner for the same reason Neuman had—to find out what I knew.

Unfortunately, or fortunately—depending on your point of view—Sam knew me better than Neuman did. He was waiting for me in the front lobby of the Rosario. He must have used his siren to get there before I did. He was furious. He gave me a choice. Either tell him everything I knew in the relative comfort of the apartment or face a charge of obstructing justice down at headquarters.

The fight lasted—off and on—for most of the rest of the evening. When he left, sometime after midnight, he knew as much as I did and we were still mad at each other. But I did have the sense to realize his anger was more concern for me than it was anything else.

What I didn't realize until much later was that I'd left out one big fact. I didn't realize it because I didn't remember it until much later.

SEVENTEEN

CONTRARY TO MY personal outlook, Thursday morning dawned clear and bright. The sky was an improbable blue, washed clean by Wednesday's storm. Driving down Queen Anne Avenue I had a panoramic view of Elliot Bay sparkling in the early morning sun. Tiny cannonball clouds dotted the horizon. Across the water the distant line of the Olympic Mountains was capped with new snow, a fitting frame for a picture-postcard scene.

I passed the Seattle Center, turned left on Denny with the Space Needle towering above me, left again on Broad and in a few minutes crossed the canal. I turned again on Bridge Way, then North 40th, and was ready to zip into the parking lot behind the office when I decided to make my rotten morning complete by going to see how far my house was from being done.

Three blocks later I heard myself make a little mewling sound of surprise as I pulled to a stop behind a commercial cleaning company's van blocking my driveway. My new windows shone with fresh-washed brilliance. All the piles of debris were gone, the porch and railings sported new coats of paint, and someone had mowed the minuscule front lawn.

Nora, my once-every-two-weeks cleaning lady, was standing in the front doorway, apparently directing operations. I had inherited Nora with the house. That is, she had been working for my great-aunt at the time and had agreed to give me a "try." We were still on that basis. Nora is younger than I, dresses better, and drives a Porsche. She also keeps my house in spotless condition, and was obviously making sure the commercial cleaning company was doing the job to her specifications.

I didn't interrupt. If Nora had put herself in charge I would soon be back in my own little nest, and from what I could see the whole place was going to be better than it was before the bomb. The morning made a 360 turnaround. I drove away singing "It's a Beautiful Morning," off-key and at the top of my lungs.

I couldn't wait to tell Martha but she was ahead of me.

"The contractor called this morning and left a message on the machine saying he was done and was sending a cleaning company out," she told me. "I called Nora."

"You're a jewel without price," I said happily.

"Don't be daft," she said, smiling. "He also said he will be sending the contract over to be signed off but I spoke to Anna and she said not to sign anything until you had inspected the finished product. Personally, I'd say let Nora do the inspecting and heaven help that contractor if it isn't done to her satisfaction."

I nodded in agreement and went skipping off into my own office. The prospect of soon moving home had me in such a euphoric daze I forgot all about my battle with Sam and had a hard time settling down to work. I was still struggling with Gregory Holbrook's life and times and was not too happy about it. We had already amassed a new and significant dossier on the man but the pivotal piece was missing. If his statement to the Hong Kong court was true and he'd been born in July 1961 in the port of Santos, Brazil, how and when had he made any connection to Grogory Maarten Holbrik who had died in Florida, in January of the previous year? Where and how had he even heard of Grogory Maarten?

Two hard hours later I had at least one of the answers. A faxed copy of Grogory Maarten Holbrik *Junior's* birth certificate. The original had obviously been done hurriedly by someone who had no reason to think that what she or he was writing would ever be of any concern. The date of birth was almost illegible as was the mother's name. The father's name—the only name of any importance in some cultures—was printed and spelled with precision. Grogory Maarten Holbrik.

Whoever had read the copy Gregory provided when he made the name change to Gregory Holbrook had simply guessed at the birth date and Gregory had either not noticed or thought it made no difference.

Under the powerful hand magnifier I kept in my desk the date was clearly 1960, not 1961, but the mother's name was still impossible to decipher. Her last name was particularly blurred. There was a possibility that Grogory, Jr., was illegitimate and it may have

bothered him enough to conceal the fact but I
wondered why, in this day and age.

On the other hand he had been born and
raised in a country where it might have made
a great deal of difference to his life. I had no
way of knowing.

I fired off another fax asking for more information and was rewarded shortly with several more faxed copies of vital statistics. These
led me to ask for several other things and by
noon I had a fairly complete picture of Gregory's life. And, unfortunately, a fairly complete picture of the mistakes I'd made, too.

The unusual name had led me so far astray
earlier on, I made doubly sure I had it right
this time before taking the whole lot down to
Anna's office.

I was going to have some apologizing to do
to Jan and his parents but I had a feeling they
would be so delighted to discover a relative,
and a reasonably close one at that, my earlier
foul-up wouldn't bother them too much. I
hoped not anyway.

Anna was a bit more cautious. "We'll see,"
she said dubiously. "I like happy endings as
well as the next guy, but first I want to know

about the money in the Swiss account." Anna, like Martha, keeps her eyes on the bottom line.

She, Martha, had some more vital stats for me when I got back to my office. She had just received a copy, from Lovington, New Mexico, of Hiram Marcus Taylor's death certificate. He died in 1937 at age fifteen, in Jal, New Mexico, thrown from a bronco in a Fourth of July rodeo.

"No wonder he never had a driver's license," I said, unaccountably saddened as I read the short, dismal record. "He was just a kid."

"And in 1950 when Bobby decided to take up a life of crime he decided to do it using Hiram's name."

I nodded. "Clever of him in a way. Certainly had me fooled."

"With one thing and another we've had half the flaming job wrong from the beginning," she said disgustedly. "And the Holbrik case, too. I wonder what else we've got wrong end up?" She flounced back to her desk muttering to herself.

I debated calling Sam to give him the stats on Hiram and then decided the heck with him. If he was so determined Tom Neuman and the

Seattle P.D. could do no wrong, he could find out for himself.

I went back to my computer and started compiling a chronological history of everything I had on the man I now knew for sure was Bobby. Robert Vernon Walker, born 1930 in Eureka, California, died a messy death two weeks ago in Seattle, Washington.

When I got to the debacle last May in Denver I stopped and I sat thinking about the Esteses, wondering why they had been in Seattle at all. After a minute I decided what the hey, she could only hang up on me, and placed a call to the blond Denver socialite.

I got a surprising response.

After I introduced myself, she said, "I wondered when someone would get around to us."

"Oh?"

"That fool Ray just wouldn't leave it alone. And it wasn't even all that much money, for heaven's sake. He loses more than that on a golf game."

"Uh…" I tried to break in but she rattled right on.

"He's just darn lucky Hiram didn't press charges. Shooting at him like that. Although I don't think he really had any intention of hit-

ting him. Actually Ray is a good shot. I think
he could of drilled him dead center if he'd
wanted to. But from the sound of things
Hiram, Bobby, whatever his name was, probably had more to hide than just bilking me out
of a thousand dollars.''

She finally paused for breath and I got a
question in. ''You did come to Seattle then to
confront Hiram, or Bobby? Whatever. How
did you know he was here?''

''Ray hired a private detective. He's been
trying to find him ever since last May. The
twit! I told him he was making a fool of himself—the blasted detective cost five times as
much as Hiram took me for—but he wouldn't
listen. So when he found out Hiram was in
Seattle he took off. And I followed him on the
next flight I could get. We always stay at the
Edgewater, I still like it better than any other
hotel in town, so I knew that's where he'd
be.''

''When did you get here?''

She laughed, a hoot of sound. Whatever else
she might be, Mrs. Estes was definitely not the
genteel type. ''Friday, the day Hiram was
killed. Isn't that a blast? Just in time to be
suspected of killing him. I've surely been sur-

prised no one wanted to talk with us yet. Not that it matters; we've both got what you might call ironclad alibis.''

''Oh? What are they?''

She laughed again. ''Ray, the idiot, was in jail all day. He arrived in Seattle on an early morning flight, hired a car, got pulled over for speeding less than a mile from the airport, tried to pull rank on the cop, and when that didn't work was stupid enough to throw a punch at him. He was arrested for drunken driving—he'd been putting them down on the plane—speeding, resisting arrest, assaulting a police officer, and a couple of other things I don't remember. When he couldn't get me at home in Denver it took the dumbhead till eight o'clock that night to figure out where I must be. After he got a hold of me at the Edgewater I went down and bailed him out. According to the newspapers I was at the cop-shop when Hiram got it.''

''It does indeed sound like you both have an ironclad,'' I agreed. ''But do you mind if I ask a couple of more questions?''

''Have at it. I don't mind.''

''How did you meet Hiram?''

''I ran into him, knocked him down in fact.

In the mall. I was in a hurry and had a bunch of packages in my arms and didn't see him. Knocked him flat on his backside. Although to tell the truth, I've wondered about that lately. He is, was, a big guy and I didn't think I hit him that hard. But he could have just been off-balance.''

I'll bet, I thought. I doubted that Hiram had ever been off-balance in his life. Until he met his killer. "Then what?" I asked.

"What?"

"What happened after you helped him to his feet? Or did you?"

"Well, of course I did. Then he helped pick up my packages, and we both apologized and...Well, one thing led to another and we ended up having a cup of coffee together. Turned out he had an intro to the same club Ray and I belong to and I saw him out there a couple of days later. We had lunch, I saw him a couple more times at the club, and then he suckered me into that darn greenback exchange. But you probably know all about that.''

"I know how he works it, yes." I knew how he worked the scam and had to admire the way he managed to meet this victim. She would never have gone for any kind of obvious pickup, but putting her in the wrong to start with gave him the perfect opening.

"Are you going to tell the cops? About us?" she asked. She didn't sound worried, just curious.

"No. Why should I? In the first place, as you say, you've both got ironclad alibis, and second, why should I do their work for them?"

She snorted with laughter. "We're in Seattle frequently. Ray has relatives there, bunch of sour apples but you don't get a choice when it comes to relatives. Next time I'm with him I'll give you a call, treat you to dinner or something. Okay? Demary Jones. Right?"

"Right. I'll look forward to it," I said, and meant it. Mrs. Estes—"call me Jo, for Josephine," she'd said—sounded like she'd be a lot of fun. I'd check their alibi to be sure, but I didn't really have any doubts. I could cross both the Esteses off my mental list of suspects. They hadn't figured very largely on it anyway. They had no connection to the Rosario.

Or did they? How did I know? Maybe that was something I needed to check out.

EIGHTEEN

I HAD NO SOONER hung up than Carol Ann called.

"Whatever did you say to Sam last night?" she demanded. "He's been roaring around here like a bull elephant all morning. Tom's lucky if he doesn't get sent back to crowd control in the boonies. Right now Sam sent him out to talk to that Mrs. Wandell, with strict orders on exactly how to approach her and even stricter orders about what he says and asks."

I had told Sam about Mrs. Wandell but I hadn't told him about Ho, the busboy, and I didn't intend to. Joey would never have forgiven me. Somehow I was going to have to figure out what to do about him on my own.

I barely put the phone down the second time when it rang again. This time it was Sam and his first words shocked me nearly speechless.

He apologized. Then of course he ruined the effect by bawling me out all over again.

"I'm sorry I yelled at you last night," he said. "But you were wrong and you have got to stay out of this investigation. You're going to get yourself killed, and what's worse, you're likely to get someone else killed, too. Probably your little friend, Joey."

That stopped me as nothing else would.

I managed to keep my voice steady as I asked him what had led him to that conclusion.

"Tom Neuman is not a total fool, Demary," he said. He sounded amused. "I'll admit he was as far as you're concerned, but he *is* competent. His mistake was grossly underestimating the information you did give him. He had his own agenda and turned a blind eye on everything else. But the fact is he has pretty much narrowed the suspect list down to the tenants of the Rosario. Which means you're in constant danger and so is anyone else fooling around that apartment."

I had to bite my tongue to keep from snapping at him. That conclusion came under the heading of, "*Well, you don't say.*" It was a conclusion I, and everyone I'd talked to, had already come to some time ago. What was frosting my cookies was that Neuman hadn't, as far as I knew, zeroed in on anyone, and he should have. With the facilities the police department had he should have been able to connect one of the tenants with Hiram/Bobby.

I was wrong about that.

Sam went on to tell me that Neuman had made the effort, actually a very exhaustive effort, but as far as they could discover there was simply no link between Hiram and anyone else living in the Rosario other than Richard Bellam, and that had turned out to be fallacious. Although it had given the crime-scene men the opportunity to go over his apartment, at least.

Without due cause they could not get a warrant to search other individual apartments for forensic evidence and with absolutely no connection between Hiram and any other tenant they were up that famous creek. They had done an exhaustive job on the halls, porch, and courtyard but hadn't come up with anything, except, of course, where the body had been lying.

"And by now any physical evidence at the murder scene itself is either long gone or so mixed with unconnected trace evidence it wouldn't be usable. If he was in one of the apartments any time at all, the perp has had plenty of time to scrub and vacuum a dozen times,'' he concluded.

"Except blood. There would have been a lot of it and they couldn't, or can't, remove all traces. You know that.''

"M-m-huh. But first we have to convince a judge we have...''

"Yes, I know, but Hiram was there, in the neighborhood, at least the one time. And probably more than once.'' I, of course, was positive he had been around, but I couldn't tell Sam how I knew, so I couldn't tell him at all. "Besides, his car was in the garage just a couple of blocks away,'' I went on. "Someone has to have seen him, and with any luck, seen him with someone from the Rosario.''

"Yes, Demary, we do know that. That's what we get paid for. We are investigating.'' he said, beginning to sound annoyed.

I decided it was time we said good-bye.

After we hung up I set my mind on how to approach Ho without involving Joey, and without alerting the killer. If, and it was a big if, the killer was the woman Hiram had dinner with. It was entirely possible the woman had nothing to do with his murder and hadn't come forward, as I'd told Joey, simply because she didn't want to get involved. She didn't necessarily live in the Rosario, either. Plus she could be married and Hiram had simply been an extramarital fling she didn't want exposed.

I still wanted her identified, but at the moment couldn't think of a practical way of doing so. What I could do, however, was go talk to Mrs. Wandell and even if she couldn't tell me anything new I could reassure her. If Neuman had upset her, which in my opinion he was likely to do.

I was wrong about that, too. I seemed to be wrong about a lot of things lately. After I introduced myself and explained why I was there she invited me in and seemed to be delighted to see me. She escorted me into her large front room. It faced the Rosario and had a window almost directly across from the apartment's front entrance. The walkway alongside the building that led to the courtyard was also clearly visible.

After I sat she insisted I have a cup of coffee, just freshly made, she said, and some of her homemade cookies. She went bustling out of the room the moment I agreed and was back within a minute or two with a tray holding a silver coffeepot, two cups and saucers, napkins, sugar and creamer, and a beautiful plate loaded with oatmeal cookies full of nuts, raisins, and candied fruit. They were delicious and so was the coffee.

Mrs. Wandell was a charming little lady, very little, in fact not even as tall as my five two, with soft blue eyes, white hair, and a plump figure. She thought being interviewed by the police was great fun.

"Although I didn't care much for that young man, Sergeant Neuman," she said thoughtfully. "He seems to have an unusually high opinion of himself."

Good for you, I thought. *You got him right.* "Were you able to tell him anything other than what you told Joey?" I asked.

"No. I didn't see anyone except the one person. And I didn't pay enough attention to him to make any kind of identification. Truthfully, I can't even say it was a him, just someone in trousers."

"Didn't you see the police cars?"

"No. Well, yes, I guess I did. I saw one car that could have been a police car but I didn't

208 DEAD MEN DIE

really look at it. My favorite program is on at
eight-thirty so I simply glanced out as I pulled
the curtains. I never heard any sirens or anything, and I don't believe I looked out the window again until I pulled the curtains open
again the next morning.''

I thought a moment. If the person she saw
had anything to do with the murder, or with
the money deposited in my account, they must
have left the Rosario between when the first
car responded to the 911 call and before any
other officers arrived. That matched the time
stamp on the deposit all right but left a very
narrow interval for the possible perp to make
the deposit and get back to the building before
he was missed. If he had come back. I still
didn't have any proof that the person who had
deposited the counterfeit in my account had
anything to do with Hiram's murder, or lived
in the Rosario.

We chatted for a while longer about the different tenants. She was full of information but
unfortunately most of it was along the lines of,
''That poor Inge Sundstrom works entirely too
hard, and not in a very nice place either. She
doesn't get home until the wee hours sometimes.''

I wondered how she knew that.

"She parks in front when she comes home late," Mrs. Wandell said. "Very sensible of her, too. At least the street is well lighted and so is the entryway. That alley is too dark for a woman to be using it in the middle of the night like last Saturday."

She did have one piece of gossip that interested me. According to her, Katherine Davis, who lived in the upstairs apartment directly opposite, "certainly has a lot of gentlemen friends."

"She doesn't bother pulling her shades, either," Mrs. Wandell confided, her eyes twinkling with amusement. "I don't make a habit of watching my neighbors," she said righteously. "But really, when you dance around hugging and kissing right in front of the window without bothering to close the drapes, you are bound to attract attention."

I grinned at her. She was apparently highly amused by Katherine's antics. Katherine was pretty young; she was in her early twenties, too young to be interested in a man as old as Hiram, but it was a possibility and I supposed I'd have to pass it on to Sam.

Later, driving back to the office, I tried to

recall who had been in the courtyard and who had not in the period between the first persons crowding around and when Neuman arrived, but my memory was too chaotic. Individual happenings, such as Ruby Chambers wiping my face with a damp cloth, Mrs. Porter from down the hall giving me a glass of water, and Mr. Johnson helping me sit down on the edge of the raised flower bed in the center of the courtyard, jumped in and out of my memory, but there was no sequence to what I remembered.

"Go get it all down on paper," Martha said when I told her. "Once you see the different incidents in black and white you may be able to sort them out into some kind of order."

She was right. I always think better when I've got a computer in front of me, and writing down everything I could remember, actually keyboarding it onto the screen, brought a lot back. None of it was clear enough, though, as far as what happened when. There had been too many people around, all of them trying to be helpful. They had undoubtedly contaminated the crime scene for the forensic team, too. No wonder Neuman had been so frustrated.

I struggled for a while trying to put what I remembered in some kind of order but it was no use. There was nearly an hour in there that simply wouldn't come clear for me. I finally gave up and instead started listing the people I knew were in the courtyard in the right time frame but there again, I couldn't get it straight. There had been too much movement. Too many people milling around, even people from the neighboring apartment buildings. Mrs. Wandell's mysterious figure might even have been from another apartment. Unlikely, though, as where would he, or she, have gotten my deposit slip?

As soon as the SOCO team got there people were moved out of the courtyard or herded into the corner by the laundry room where the media was confined, but that first twenty minutes or so after I fell over Hiram and Inge opened the hall door had been too confusing for me to sort into any kind of arrangement.

"In a way, that's good," Martha said thoughtfully when I told her.

"It is?"

"Yes. Look at it this way. If the killer was in the courtyard when you drove in he could have mixed with the crowd without any trouble. No one would have noticed him particularly.''

"So?''

"So if he wasn't a total clod he would have realized you hadn't seen him and didn't know diddly. And now that I think about it, we should have caught on to that a lot sooner. It's been two weeks tomorrow. If the killer had any thought of you being a danger to him he's had ample opportunity to do something about it. He hasn't, so it stands to reason he realizes you aren't a danger to him.'' She stopped and stared at me for a moment. "Well, that's not entirely true; you are a threat to him, but he's not to know that. Unless he's someone who knows you and knows you're looking for him, that is.''

That was reassuring. In a way. Maybe.

NINETEEN

FRIDAY WASN'T a "business as usual" day. It started off with what Martha called "the blooming contractor" and Nora arriving at shortly after nine. Nora with a clipboard in her hand and the contractor with a scowl on his face. The contractor demanding to know what business this woman had interfering in his affairs, and Nora, shoving the clipboard under his nose, telling him he'd either rectify the problems she'd listed or he was not only not going to be paid, his license was going to be in serious jeopardy.

The problems were two warped hardwood planks in the room above the front hall, a cracked cornice in my bedroom, and two other similar items Nora was insisting be repaired. Immediately.

The problems were more or less solved when Anna Carmine showed up—Martha had called her—and took the two of them down the hall to her office. The contractor left fifteen minutes later looking chastened, followed by Nora looking well satisfied.

"It will take at least two weeks for that man to get the planks to repair the floor, but he'll have the rest of it done this afternoon," she told me. "You can go ahead and move back in tomorrow, but Anna says he is not to be paid off until the floor is done."

I nodded, somewhat awestruck. I'm no slouch when it comes to defending my territory but Nora has me beat by a mile.

I had no sooner settled down after that uproar than Sean called and asked me to be very careful what I said to Edith, and particularly not to mention him to her.

"All right," I said, "I won't—mention you, I mean—but why?"

He hemmed and hawed but finally told me. "Edie Vammen, known at the moment as Edith Vibike, is an Israeli bank examiner. She is here with the full knowledge of the State Department and I'd very much prefer her not to know I even exist. And I particularly don't want her knowing I was looking into any of her accounts. As you know, I was skating close to the edge on that one.''

I gulped air. Fluffy-headed Edith, a bank examiner? Boy, when I guessed wrong I really guessed wrong. Or had I? Being a bank examiner didn't preclude being a killer. There had been a number of banker/villains in the past, and Edith definitely fit my mental profile of Hiram's victims.

After we hung up I sat staring at the wall, thinking. What in the world was an Israeli bank examiner doing in Seattle? And did it have any bearing on Hiram's death? When Martha came in with the mail I asked her to sit for a minute. I wanted to run an idea by her.

''What idea?'' she asked, twitching the mariner's compass wall hanging as she sat. I'd forgotten to change back to the flame-colored one and I guessed I'd better hurry up and do it while this one still had some shape left.

''I'm beginning to think Edith dumped that money on me,'' I said baldly.

''Edith? What in the world gives you that idea? Why would she do it?''

''Because she killed Hiram. She's one of the few people in the apartment who knows I have a P.I. license, and I think the deposit was meant to throw me off track.''

She stared at me as if I'd just turned green. ''Well, you're the detective,'' she said finally. ''But I don't follow that at all. She wasn't even there that night.''

''She could have been. She was supposed to leave that morning but there is no proof that she did. And given Edith's wooly thinking I believe it could have happened, despite her being a bank examiner.''

''A bank examiner?'' Martha's voice rose to a squeak. ''Whatever are you talking about?''

I explained Sean's call.

''Stone the crows! Now that is one for the books,'' she said, looking even more astounded.

''There's no other explanation I can think of. It, the deposit, didn't accomplish anything except to draw my attention away from the murder, and she could well be in possession of counterfeit.''

''But that means you think she killed Hiram. Why?''

''I still have some gaps but I think it went like this,'' I said slowly, thinking it out as I went along. "Bobby's bank balance had been dropping steadily for several months. His July balance hit an all-time low, so he assumed his Hiram identity and came to Seattle to replenish his cash supply. He checked into a good hotel, rented a big car, and set out to pick his mark."

"Edith? But how…"

"I haven't a clue how he met her but by the time he was killed his scheme must have been all set to go, and it must have involved a trip of some kind. He checked out of the Edgewater that morning—Tom Neuman established that early on—but kept his rental car. He wouldn't have kept the car if he'd been going back to Eureka."

"Why not? He may have meant to turn it in at the airport."

"Possible, of course, but the hotel has an airport shuttle that is a heck of a lot more convenient. Plus, it was found in a garage less than two blocks from the apartment. I think he needed it at the apartment to set up his trip scam. At any rate, in my scenario he goes to Edith's apartment—remember she told me several days earlier that she was going to be gone for a while?—but somehow he makes a mistake and she realizes what's going down.

She kills him, removes his clothes to delay identification, cleans up the mess, and carries him outside, meaning to take his body somewhere else to dispose of. Maybe just to the Dumpster where it could have stayed for who knows how long before anyone discovered him. But then, just as she gets to the porch, I come driving in so she's forced to leave him on the porch and get back into her own place.''

"Have you any proof? Any at all?''

''No, and I know it's got a lot of holes, but it's a good working hypothesis. I'm sure she's guilty—she practically told me why she took his clothes—and she fits Bobby/Hiram's M.O. like it was made for her. She matches the description of the woman he was with at the Cornerpost, is capable of carrying him from her apartment to the porch—it's only about twenty feet from her door and she's strong, all those workouts she does every morning—and she could have gotten one of my deposit slips any time. Last but not least, she has a substantial bank account. That's the one thing Hiram would have made sure of before he picked his mark. Also, she supposedly left Seattle early in the morning but she didn't check into the

Golden Lion Motel in Portland until three the following morning.''

"If she was trying to establish an alibi, why did she only go as far as Portland?'' she asked. She thought for a moment. "I'm going to get a hold of the gal I talked to down there right away and check on that,'' she said, frowning. "But to go back, how did she get away from the apartment without being seen?''

"Several ways. She could have been the person Mrs. Wandell saw. She could have had her car parked a couple of blocks away, deposited the money, and just kept right on going. Or she could have simply waited in her place until it calmed down some and then walked out. With all the commotion going on it would have been easy enough. Or she could have been going out the front door while I was stumbling around in her flower garden.''

Martha shook her head. "I don't know, it sounds pretty thin to me. Remember we're talking murder here. Wouldn't she have been more likely to simply start yelling for the cops when she caught on to him? I would.''

"Maybe she didn't want to blow her cover. For whatever she's doing here.''

"I thought you liked her.''

"I do like her, and I don't think she planned on killing him. May not have meant to, either. I think she just got mad and hit him with something."

"With what? Has she got something in her apartment that fits the forensic report? Does she collect antique maces or something?"

"I don't know what it was. Not yet anyway."

"What does Sam think about this hypothesis?"

I made a face. "I haven't mentioned it to him. I know it's thin; I just put it together this morning. I haven't had a chance to do any checking, but it does fit."

"Well, I'd say you better do some really serious checking before you tell him or anyone else. It not only sounds thin, it sounds libelous to me," she said, getting up to return to her own desk.

Fortunately for my reputation as a "detective," I agreed with her. It was just a theory and I wasn't about to share it with anyone else without some substantial proof. Certainly not with Sam.

Lunchtime came and went while I worked on an overdue report for one of my insurance company clients. It wasn't particularly tricky but it was long and involved, plus I rechecked everything to make doubly sure I had all the case numbers and the corresponding evidence files included. I had made so many mistakes lately I was getting paranoid about making sure I had things right.

I was packing the whole lot up and was ready to call the messenger service, when Martha came in looking flustered.

"Demary, Anna needs you in her office. Right away. I don't know what's happening but I could hear a regular bedlam going on behind her when she phoned."

I took off on the fly. It wasn't like Anna to call for help.

TWENTY

I COULD HEAR the row going on before I was halfway down the hall. There didn't seem to be anything really violent happening, however, no real screaming or furniture breaking. I heard Jodie exhorting someone to "put a sock in it."

Anna's office was full to capacity. All the Holbriks were there, including Jan's wife, Esther, and their two children who were sitting on a couch against the wall, their eyes as big as silver dollars as they took in the happy cries, tears, and general commotion going on around them. Everyone appeared to be in a high state of emotion, either deliriously happy or suffering from hysterics. Anna and Jodie were doing their best to calm things down but without notable success.

At first I couldn't figure what had started the hubbub, but after a second look around it was pretty obvious. If all the men in the room hadn't come out of the same gene pool, I'd be greatly surprised. Paul and Gregory looked so much alike that even with the age difference they could have been brothers, rather than the uncle and nephew they undoubtedly were. Even Jan's small son's features were almost a carbon copy of Gregory Holbrook's. Whatever else Gregory might be, he was certainly a family member.

When we finally got all the happy tears mopped up and everyone in a more composed frame of mind, Anna began explaining what had happened, how she'd contacted Gregory, and why she'd invited everyone here to her office. Like the good lawyer she was, she started at the very beginning, saying that any individual comments or questions could be added as we went along.

"I think we can all agree on accepting Demary's findings and Paul's memory of what his uncle Carl told him, at least up to the point where Gregory Maartin and cousin Carl parted company in Marseilles in November of 1939. Right?" She looked around, eyebrows raised in query. Everybody nodded.

Paul and Marti were holding hands so

tightly it was a wonder they didn't cut off each other's circulation, but they were smiling happily.

"Now, our next point of interest is how did Grogory arrive in Brazil and when? Do you know?" She looked at Gregory.

"Of my own knowledge, no I don't, only what I was told and that not much. I'll have to fall back a bit to tell you why. All right?" He looked around, received nods of agreement, and went on. "My mother died less than three years after I was born. She was a German Jewess who had escaped, as a baby with her parents, to Argentina in the early thirties. She met and married my father there in 1956, but how he arrived there and how they met I never heard. Later on, they moved to Rio de Janeiro."

No wonder I hadn't been able to trace a marriage license in Brazil.

"My father had already been there sometime, though, and had established himself as a banking authority, so when the Israelis started making problems for the German expatriates in Rio he decided to get my mother away from there. Not that her family had ever been Nazis, but they were full-blooded German. He obtained a job in São Paulo, and later other members of her family, including a sister and her husband, moved to Brazil also. My father intended the move as a temporary stopgap while he made efforts to obtain United States citizenship. He went there, to the United States, in early 1960 to see about applying for temporary residency. And as you know, he died there, in Miami.''

He stopped and looked around. ''You realize all this is hearsay. All of it told to me by my aunt and uncle who took me in when my mother died.''

''How old were you then? Do you remember her?'' Anna asked.

Paul and Marti were wiping tears from their faces, no doubt thinking of this long-lost little nephew they would have loved to have raised with Jan.

Gregory shook his head. ''I was three years old and have no personal memory of her at all. My aunt, who I regarded as my mother all of the rest of her life, had one small snapshot of her sister. I still have it. It's the only link I have with her.''

''What prompted you to move to Australia?'' I asked.

He smiled. "It wasn't my decision. My aunt and uncle decided to emigrate there and as they had ample money to do so, we went. I was fifteen. I never cared much for the country, mostly, I think, because it was so different from Santos, where I'd been raised and had friends. When both my aunt and uncle were gone and I was alone, they'd had no children, I moved on. To Hong Kong first and recently here to Vancouver." He gave the assembled Holbriks a watery smile. "I never dreamed I'd find a family here. I'd always understood from my aunt that none of my father's people had escaped Austria."

"You have no wife?" Marti asked anxiously.

He shook his head. "Good Jewish girls are scarce in Hong Kong," he said, trying for a note of humor.

"Any questions?" Anna asked, looking around. No one responded, so she went on, "All right then, we get now to the next point. The money in the Swiss bank account."

Jan and family looked at Gregory. He looked totally blank.

"What money?" he asked. "As a banker I know about the Holocaust assets held by the

Swiss banks, but only in general. Are you saying there is family money there? The Crédit Suisse agreed to a settlement last August. Have you filed a claim? Do you have any papers? Do you know the account numbers?''

"No, we have nothing but a letter telling us the money was being deposited. Your father was the family money man,'' Paul said gently. "That was his job. And as far as we know, or can guess, he was carrying the proofs with him in a metal attaché case when he left Marseilles. Do you remember ever seeing it?''

Gregory looked back and forth at the other men, an appalled expression washing across his face. Anna leaned back in her chair, her chin on her steepled fingers. Jodie, eyes dancing, tried to look at everyone at once.

"I never saw my father, let alone his attaché case,'' he said, his voice strained. "Did you expect me to know about…Do you think I…''

"No, no, no.'' Marti cried. "It would be nice if you did know about the money but the money isn't why we looked for you, and we are so happy to have found you. We're family, that's what's important.''

Anna gave me a skeptical glance but didn't

interrupt the excited discussion that had broken out again among the Holbriks.

I gathered from the snippets of talk I could make out that Gregory had already done considerable work for other Holocaust claimants and now proposed to do the same for this, his own family. The whole group, except the two children who appeared to have fallen asleep in the midst of it all, were all so happy with one another, I began to have a good feeling about it myself. For once I seemed to have done something right.

I didn't see as they needed me so I slipped out while they were still happily engaged in sorting family members for Gregory's benefit. I'd done a family tree for Jan, so I knew just how many lost aunts, uncles and cousins Gregory would now hear about.

Martha met me halfway along the hall. "Well? I knew it wasn't a knockdown fight when the noise died down, but...?"

I smiled, still feeling good about the Holbriks. "I'd say it was more of a lovefest than anything else. They're so happy, all of them, to find a family member, it's enough to make me start believing in Santa Claus again."

Martha shivered. "When I hear about people like the Holbriks and think about all those others who died in Hitler's death camps, whole families wiped out, it makes me want to shake the stuffing out of those neo-Nazi ruffians, to do something to make sure the world never forgets, never lets it happen again.''

I nodded, agreeing wholeheartedly.

A HALF HOUR LATER Martha marched into my office with a very different attitude. ''I hope you haven't confided your Edith pipe dream to anyone,'' she said sharply.

I scowled at her. ''No, I haven't. But what makes you think it's such a pipe dream?'' I demanded. ''It fits the facts.''

''Except for one little glitch. She actually arrived at the Golden Lion in Portland shortly after eleven, and was seen having dinner in the dining room, with what my mate down there described as a very handsome man. They lingered in the lounge until after two when Edith went to sign the registration card and go up to her room. Which pretty well shoots down your attempt to fit her into the murder scene.''

I rubbed my eyes, thinking. ''Not necessarily. If she left the apartment at or around eight-thirty, she could have been in Portland by eleven without any trouble. No, I'll admit I could be wrong, but she's still in the frame. This information doesn't change anything."

Martha growled at me and went back to her desk. As she had never ever seen Edith I couldn't imagine why she was defending her so forcefully.

I decided I needed something to eat, got my coat and headed for Julia's, always my first choice when it comes to food, but changed my mind before I got there and headed instead for the Pike Street Public Market. I love the Market. Not only is it colorful with the vegetables, fruits, flowers, fish, and whatever, all laid out in gleaming displays to tempt the shoppers, the people who frequent the market are a constantly changing delight. Market customers are what some famous Seattle author once called a multifaceted slice of the Northwest lifestyle.

I thought being there might take my mind off the mixed-up mess Hiram's death was beginning to assume in my head, but no such luck. I had no sooner parked the Toyota and was walking down the hill past Sur La Table, the kitchenware shop, when I spotted Carol Ann across the street, her arms loaded with sacks of fresh vegetables and a loaf of De-

Laurenti's sourdough French bread. She saw
me at the same time and called to me to wait
until she'd stowed her purchases in her car—
she pointed just up the hill—and then we
could have coffee together.

I agreed, although I intended to eat, too, and
a few minutes later we sat down in a pasta
place I liked in Post Alley.

I ordered a bowl of fresh-made fettuccine in
white clam sauce, a radicchio salad with olive
oil and balsamic vinegar, and a glass of rasp-
berry iced tea.

Carol Anne said she wasn't going to sit
there and drool while I ate, and ordered the
same.

"Well, how's the Wallingford sleuth doing?" she asked after the waitress left. "Got
ol' Hiram's death all figured out?"

"What I've got is a strong desire to forget
the whole thing," I told her truthfully.

"If I believed that I'd be looking for lep-
rechauns under the Fremont Bridge," she said,
laughing.

"I don't have a client and I don't see why
I should do the Seattle P.D.'s work for them,"
I said petulantly.

Her smile faded into a surprised expression.

"You're ticked off about something, aren't you?" she said. "If nothing else I'd think you'd want to find him for your own benefit, before he decides to off you, too. That's what's bothering Sam, anyway."

"He said that?"

She shrugged. "No, of course not, but I've been working with him almost as long as you two have been sniping at each other. I know him, and I know how worried he is. He's afraid the perp will try to take you out before he can get a handle on him."

I explained Martha's, and my, thought about that, but Carol Ann shook her head, disagreeing.

"You know better than that, Demary. Agreed, he may have realized that first evening that you hadn't seen him, but by now he knows you're looking, and also knows you have the best chance of finding him. He's still a danger to you. Maybe more than he was to start with."

"How do you figure?"

"You're not thinking the perp was that old cliché, the wandering maniac, are you?"

"Don't be silly."

"Well then, he—or she—is someone familiar with the Rosario. Right?"

"Yes, of course."

"You know the Rosario, you know the people, you were there. Sooner or later something is going to go 'click' in your head and you'll have him targeted. And unless he's a total idiot, he knows that. Ergo, he's going to get you if he can."

I suddenly lost my appetite and was back where I was that first night. Scared.

TWENTY-ONE

AFTER I LEFT Carol Ann I drove back to the office, told Martha I was through for the day, and headed for the apartment to pack up the few clothes and things I'd taken over there. It was already getting dark, the courtyard gloomy and filled with shadows, so I ended up just stuffing clothes in my suitcase and filling a couple of shopping bags with the odds and ends I'd picked up in the past month. I'd gotten over the first chill of fright that shook me listening to Carol Ann, but I didn't feel confident enough to be carrying stuff out to my car in the dark. I had lingered in the office long enough to unearth the .32 I'd finally remembered hiding underneath a stack of old files at the back of a cabinet, but I don't like guns, and having it in my purse didn't make me feel any safer.

When I had everything packed except my

pajamas and what I'd need the next day, I
went to bed. I'd picked up the new Tony Hill-
erman at the bookstore in the Interlake Mall
the day before and although it was still early
evening, going to bed with a cup of hot choc-
olate and a good book had a nice sound to it.
In fact I had such a comfy, safe feeling I ended
up asleep long before I would have thought
possible.

MORNING SHOWED yesterday's vapors up as
the silliness they were. Whether anything ever
went "click" in my head or not, I doubted
anyone was out to get me. I swallowed a cup
of coffee, tossed everything I'd packed into
the backseat of the Toyota, and I set off for
my own house in a glow of pleasure. I'd have
to go back one more time to do a few last-
minute cleaning chores, but then I'd be out of
the Rosario for good. Actually it was a very
nice residence, several cuts above the average
apartment, but I wouldn't be sorry to see the
last of the place.

Joey was sitting on my porch steps when I
pulled into the drive. He carted everything into
the house and inspected the repairs for flaws.
I was glad to see him and it felt so good to be

home I almost hated to protest when he told me what he wanted me to do.

He wanted Ho to take a look at every woman living in the Rosario and had finally figured out a way to do it without alerting them to what he was really doing. He told me he and Ho were going to go door to door to offer a well-known brand of cleaning powder, at below the regular cost, to raise money for the Disue relief fund, and he needed me to print out a dozen or so flyers extolling the fund and the product's superior capabilities.

"You can just copy what they say on the can for most of it," he told me. "I'd do it myself but our printer don't have good graphics capabilities and I want a real classy-looking sheet to hand them. Something to make it look legit."

"Joey, you can't do that," I said, vexed with him. He knew better. "In the first place, what's this Disue relief fund? You can't go collecting money for something that doesn't exist. It's illegal."

He gave me one of his affronted looks. "Disue is something Ho's mother cooks—I think it's some kind of soup. It's the only word I could think of that sounded like a disease Ho might have, and we aren't going to collect any money. I got better sense than that. We're going to hand them the cleanser and the printout, tell them someone else will be along later to collect, and be on our way. All we want to do is get a look at the women. There's only seven of them who fit Ho's description and I already scoped out the apartment numbers so we won't be in the place a half hour.''

Actually, it was a pretty good idea, but I didn't like it anyway. ''What makes you think they'll believe you?''

He grinned. ''Ho's going to dress up in some clothes his sister brought from Saigon. He says it's what most of the women wear over there. It looks kinda like the outfits the nuns used to wear. White pants and a white dress thing that hangs clear to the floor, and with his head shaved, he'll look like he's dying of something for sure.''

''His head shaved?'' I goggled at him, completely nonplussed. ''His folks said that would be all right?''

''Sure, why not? It'll grow back.''

I couldn't imagine how he'd persuaded Ho, or his family, to go along with the head shav-

ing, but Joey's powers of persuasion are nothing if not amazing.

I made up the flyers to his specifications.

The fund-raising/identification event was
scheduled to take place at three that afternoon.
I promised to be on hand, in my apartment, in
case of need. Actually I insisted on being
there. Joey didn't see any need for me but
agreed to let me know the results as soon as
they were in.

AT A QUARTER OF THREE, parking my car in
the Rosario garage, I remembered I'd left my
iron in the laundry room so I went over there
first. I needed to retrieve it before someone
decided it was fair game. They don't have
much trouble that way around the Rosario, but
still...

I was recrossing the patio with the iron,
swinging my arm back and forth like a pen-
dulum, when I suddenly knew what had killed
Hiram.

*A smooth, arrow-shaped blunt instrument
measuring four to five inches at its widest
point.*

Hiram had been killed with an iron!
Brought down point-first with any force at all

it was certainly heavy enough to have stunned him even if the blow hadn't hit his temple, which it had. The two blows that smashed his skull could have been made after he was unconscious.

I forgot all about being mad at Sam and called him at home.

"Sam, I think I know how Hiram was killed," I told him, sounding as casual as possible. "And maybe *who*."

"You think you know who the murderer is?" Sam did not sound casual. He sounded angry, or maybe frightened. That idea flustered me.

"I think so," I said slowly. I started to tell him what I thought, but he interrupted me.

"Where are you? At home?"

"No, I'm at the apartment."

"All right, Demary, now you listen to me. I want you to lock your door and stay inside. Don't let anyone in. No one. You hear me? I'll be there in fifteen minutes and you can tell me all about it then. Okay?"

For a second I was tempted to tell him to forget it—I hate it when he tries to boss me around—but I was too anxious about the iron. I wanted him to get a warrant and get a hold of the thing before she got rid of it, if she hadn't already.

"Oh, all right," I said finally. "But hurry up, will you? I want to get this over with."

I had just put the phone down and was taking off my coat when Inge knocked on my door.

"It's me, Inge," she called. "Can I borrow some coffee? I don't have enough for breakfast tomorrow and I'm too darn tired to go to the store."

"Sure." I snapped the bolt back and let her in. "What kind do you want? Ground or instant?"

"Instant will be fine, thanks. Just enough to get me going in the morning. I'll stop at the store on my way home."

She followed me to the kitchen and handed me a paper cup as I got the jar out of the cupboard.

"How about having some now?" I asked. Sam's attitude had made me nervous about being alone. "I'll make a pot."

She shook her head no, then said, "Okay. Why not. It's still early enough not to bother me. Plus I just pulled a shift and a half. I don't think I'll have any trouble sleeping tonight."

I put the water on for coffee and we wandered back into the living room talking about the manager's new laundry room schedule. It had half of the tenants doing their washing in the middle of the night. Fortunately no one paid much attention to his edicts. Inge sat down as I went over to pull the shades. It was so gray out it seemed like it should be evening.

Edith was coming across the patio. She was annoyed about something; I could tell by the way she stomped up onto the landing and tugged at the back door, trying to force the automatic closing device beyond its designed speed. It shrieked viciously, resisting her efforts.

The sound echoed in my memory. I'd heard that metallic scream just minutes before I'd fallen over Hiram's body.

Then it hit me.

The noise I'd heard that night had been short and sharp. Whoever had been opening or closing the door, it hadn't been Edith. She wasn't strong enough to force the device shut that quickly.

Inge had told Tom Neuman she heard me yell, raced out of her apartment, down the stairs, and opened the door to find me fighting my way out of the bushes. Three minutes.

When she opened the door I was trying to get out of the shrubbery all right, but it hadn't been three minutes. It had been more like thirty seconds. I hadn't even thought about that particular time frame before but I did now, and I knew. Inge hadn't come from her apartment. She had been on the other side of the door she had just forced to close in a fraction of its usual time.

She was tall, strong, blond, and had a substantial bank account. She could have picked up one of my deposit slips the day I'd dropped my trash in the patio.

Edith hadn't killed Hiram, Inge had.

I couldn't have hesitated more than thirty seconds before I dropped the curtain cord and turned away from the window, toward the table, my purse, and the .32 inside it, but my expression must have given me away. Before I had gone three steps toward the table Inge was across the room. She grabbed my arm and twisted it into a kind of half nelson that nearly paralyzed me.

"If you try anything I'll kill you right here," she said, her voice coolly matter-of-

fact. "We use this hold to subdue mental pa-
tients when they run amok." She made a
sound somewhere between a snort and a laugh.
"The so-called death-hold. Now walk slowly,
carefully, back over to the window and pull
the drapes closed."

"I can't," I gasped. "I can't move."

She gave my arm a tug. Pain shot down my
spine.

"Yes you can. I told you, this is a common
hold used in psychiatric care. I know exactly
what you can do, and exactly how much force
I need to persuade you. Now, walk." She gave
my arm another little jerk.

I walked, slowly and carefully, over to the
window, praying with every painful step she
wouldn't remember I hadn't locked the door
again after she came in. Sam would be here
soon. It had already been at least ten minutes
since I'd phoned him. All I had to do was keep
her from killing me until he got there. Because
that's what she intended. She didn't need to
tell me, I could see it on her face.

I couldn't get away from her. The hold she
was using had undoubtedly been designed to
control someone a lot larger and stronger than

I was. The only thing I had control of was my head, and I knew I'd better use it.

"Why, Inge? Why did you kill him?" I asked, forcing the words past the fear that clogged my throat.

"None of your business," she said harshly. "Now move over to the hall. We're going into the bedroom."

I moved. I didn't have any choice. "At least tell me why you deposited the money in my account. The Treasury man thinks I'm part of a counterfeit gang." Sean didn't, of course, but anything to keep her mind off snapping my neck.

She laughed shortly. "Seemed like a good idea at the time. There wasn't any place to burn it, and one of your deposit slips was still in the wastebasket beside my desk from when I'd helped you and Edith pick up your trash a couple of weeks before. You needed something to keep your mind off anything you might have seen that night."

"But how did you do it? The deposit was time stamped eight-thirty. The police were here then. How did you get past them?"

"They weren't interested in me. When I came back downstairs from changing my dress

I simply walked out the front door, went over to the bank—it's only three blocks—came back and rejoined the crowd. Nobody noticed. And if they had I'd have said I needed some air.''

"Hiram was pulling some kind of a con game on you with that money, wasn't he?

"He thought he was." She made a harsh, angry sound as she remembered. "We were going to Reno for the weekend. I was pressing a dress when he showed me that wad of hundreds. Said he'd made a cash sale and didn't want to be carrying that many bills around. He wanted me to deposit it in my account until we got back, to drop it in the automatic teller machine. As if I couldn't recognize fake when I saw it. He'd have asked me for a check, just to secure his money, of course, then cashed it and been long gone. I told him..." She stopped, breathing heavily in my ear.

"You were washing Hiram's clothes that day I met you in the laundry room, weren't you?" I asked quickly. "What did you do with them, anyway?"

"Dumped them in a Goodwill collection box."

"All his clothes? And his suitcase?"

She shrugged, loosening her hold a fraction. "Why not? I took care of all identifying marks. I didn't want to leave them in the car. If that fool drama critic in the garage hadn't insisted on helping me carry the suitcase down the stairs he—"

Someone knocked on my door.

I didn't hesitate. I brought my heel down on her instep with all the force I could muster, threw myself in the direction opposite her hold, and screamed. I'd like to say I used my karate skills to bring her under control. Unfortunately I don't know karate from a kick in the shins. What I had was sheer dumb luck, and I had on a heavy pair of Doc Martens. I broke seven bones in her foot. The shock sent her lurching into the coffee table where she grabbed for the pole light to steady herself, missed, and fell flat on her face. I jumped, got both hands in her hair, and was banging her face into the carpet when Joey and Ho came charging in and joined the fray. Sam, just minutes behind them, dragged us all apart and snapped the cuffs on a disheveled and raging Inge.

Ho danced around screaming, "It's her, it's her!"

Joey looked smug.

AT NINE O'CLOCK that night, still comfortably groggy from the painkillers the orthopedic surgeon used when he set my little finger—I'd broken it myself banging Inge's head on the floor—I sat back in the hospital examining chair and listened to Sam recap the case.

"Okay, have I got it all now?" he asked, looking up from his notebook. "She talked some before we booked her but I'd like to be sure you haven't forgotten some other little thing."

I hoped he wasn't going to bawl me out again. He'd already done that at least four times.

I nodded. "That's everything I know. In fact, right up to the time you got there and separated the four of us, if she'd simply turned around and walked out I couldn't have proved a thing. I should have figured it out long ago when I remembered her sticking so close to me the night of the murder. I thought she was trying to protect me, but of course it wasn't that at all. She was making sure I hadn't seen her before she got the door shut.

"The malpractice suit in Wyoming prompted me to check her bank balance.It's plenty hefty, so she must have won the case, but that didn't mean anything. All I really had was that she was tall, blond, and matched the description of the woman seen with Hiram at the Cornerpost. There were the man's clothes she washed, of course, but..." I shrugged. "Did she tell you how she met him? And did you get her iron?"

"Yes to both questions. The lab has the iron. We won't know for sure until they're through with it, but I'm pretty sure you're right about it being the murder weapon. She met him at the clinic. He cut his finger on a piece of broken glass and went there to have it stitched. Actually, he may have cut it on purpose, to give him an excuse to meet her. We'll never know.

"Hiram was in Cheyenne at the time the malpractice suit was going on. He was pulled in and questioned about a family Bible scam. He may have read or heard about the case and had her in mind ever since."

"Could be. I wonder if she knows where Hiram got the counterfeit money?"

"I doubt it, but I talked to your friend McBride a couple of hours ago and he thinks now that Hiram simply bought it. Both the hundreds and the twenties. The hundreds to use in his scam, and the twenties to stretch his working capital. Normally the hundreds would only have had to pass for the few seconds he'd let the mark see them. It was his bad luck that Inge was good at spotting counterfeit. Oh, McBride asked me to tell you he's gone up a notch in his boss's estimation and to say 'good-bye'; he's leaving in the morning for El Paso to investigate another bunch of bills from the same plates.''

I could see Sam wanted to know what that was about, but I wasn't going to tell him. He didn't need to know everything. Besides, I was getting tired and there was one more loose end I wanted to tie down. I asked, "Did you call Portland and find out anything about what Edith was doing down there?''

Sam chuckled. "Yes. Your nice, scatty, little blond neighbor is not only a bank examiner, she's a highly respected Israeli agent, and believe it or not the two of you have been working on practically parallel lines.''

"What line? I'm not...''

"You've been tracing a Jewish banker, Gregory Holbrook, haven't you?''

"Yes, but...

"She's been after him, or actually his father, for nearly a year. She got the two men mixed up, pretty much the same way you did. The father was a suspected Nazi, or at least she thought he was a party member, and you just blew her case for her. Austrian Jews weren't party members. Never. She's not a happy camper, believe me. She went to Portland to confer with another agent before taking a week's vacation; she was telling the truth about that, anyway. By the time she got back you had the Holbrook case pretty well sorted. Left her looking a fool." He grinned. "You had her wrong, Demary, but on the other hand, she was really wrong about you."

"Wrong about me? How?" I scowled. I didn't like the way he was grinning at me. "What was she thinking about me?"

"Well, I hate to tell you this, Demary, but she had you pegged for a real airhead. She knew you were a P.I. and even knew you were working for Jan Holbrik. She just didn't think you had the brains to trace Holbrook. How's that for brightening your day?"

Sam was still laughing when the doctor came back to tell me I could go home.

I didn't think it was all that funny.

CRIMES OF

Passion

Sometimes Cupid's aim can be deadly...

FIRE AND ICE

As a severe ice storm strikes northern Vermont,
Ruth Willmarth is drawn into the murder investigation
of a young woman stabbed with a massive icicle,
in a mystery filled with dark secrets of the heart.

NIGHT FLAMES

When a wealthy land developer's house goes up in flames
on Valentine's night, killing its owner, Oklahoma City
police detective Jennifer Weathers picks through a crime
scene littered with red heart-shaped balloons.

ST. VALENTINE'S DIAMOND

Hoping that a diamond for Valentine's Day will convince his
beloved Fidelma to be his wife, Danny O'Flaherty goes to see
an old friend in Manhattan's diamond district. The visit turns
into a St. Valentine's Day massacre when he returns home—
to find a corpse on his bed.

THE LOVEBIRDS

What do you give a mistress for Valentine's Day? In the case
of Peggy Kane, an expensive box of chocolates loaded with
poison. Hotel detective Tempest Bailey suspects there's more
to this romantic tragedy than just desserts.

Available January 2002 at your favorite retail outlet.

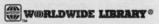 **W⊕RLDWIDE LIBRARY** ®

W407

STEVEN F. HAVILL

DEAD

A SHERIFF BILL GASTNER MYSTERY

WEIGHT

Sheriff Bill Gastner knows his Posadas, New Mexico, territory. So when a backhoe crushes a man to death, it's more instinct than fact that leaves him feeling there's more to this "accident" than meets the eye.

Adding to his problems, anonymous letters charging his best deputy with hustling Mexican nationals for cash are being dispatched around town. Gastner takes this one personally; he's fond of his deputy, but he wants the truth. He also knows it's an election year and dirty politics can happen anywhere. So can murder.

Soon he's got not just one, but two dead bodies. And a strong desire to make sure that when he does retire...it's not by way of a well-aimed bullet.

Available January 2002 at your favorite retail outlet.

 WORLDWIDE LIBRARY ®   W408

KILLER

A Charlie Greene Mystery

COMMUTE

California literary agent Charlie Greene starts her weeklong vacation by shutting off the phone, putting out the cat—and finding the body of her neighbor slumped in his SUV. With nothing but her track record for stumbling onto bodies to incriminate her, Charlie becomes the prime suspect.

It seems as if Charlie's dearly departed neighbor had some dangerous secrets involving bundles of hidden cash. Soon a strategically placed bomb, a temporary loss of hearing, a stint in jail—all topped off by the stunning events unfolding in her own backyard—lead Charlie to the inescapable conclusion that vacations really are murder.

"...clever and original plotting..."
—*Publishers Weekly*

MARLYS MILLHISER

Available December 2001 at your favorite retail outlet.

WMM405

Linda Berry

DEATH AND THE HUBCAP

A Trudy Roundtree Mystery

Though the town of Ogeechee isn't far from bustling Atlanta, it still retains the charm and quirks of some sleepy Southern communities. Topping that list is Tanner Whitcomb, who drives through town in an imaginary car with a hubcap for a steering wheel. So when he reports that he's run over somebody, officer Trudy Roundtree puts on a straight face and goes to investigate.

She finds a dead body with a tire mark on it.

Putting Tanner's claims of guilt aside, Trudy follows a trail, where even her own past becomes part of the complex mystery as she closes in on a killer who is more than willing to kill again.

"This is a fun-to-read, down home regional mystery... provides insight into life in a small Georgia town..."
—*The Midwest Book Review*

Available January 2002 at your favorite retail outlet.

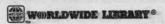WORLDWIDE LIBRARY®